ORACLES

ORACLES
A NOVEL

Melissa Tantaquidgeon Zobel

University of New Mexico Press | ALBUQUERQUE

Library of Congress Cataloging-in-Publication Data

Zobel, Melissa Tantaquidgeon, 1960–
   Oracles : a novel / Melissa Tantaquidgeon Zobel.—1st ed.
      p. cm.
   ISBN 0-8263-3191-2 (alk. paper)
   1. Indians of North America—Fiction.
   2. Women shamans—Fiction.
   I. Title.
PS3626.024 O73 2004
813'.6—dc22
                                    2003020182

Illustrations: ©Aaron Dewick, Little People LLC

Design and composition: Melissa Tandysh

SPECIAL THANKS
TO
MY COUSINS

SANDRA EICHELBERG, who suggested the name "Yantuck" for the tribe in this book. As the Mohegan Tribe's Enrollment Coordinator, she encountered so many make-pretend tribes that she easily invented yet another.

ANITA FOWLER, Director of Little People, LLC, who constantly reminds the world that her grandfather (Chief Little Hatchet) was right about the Giants and Little People of New England.

JOSEPH SMITH, who brought home to the Hill more gifts than he will ever know.

AND

STACY DUFRESNE & SANDI PINEAULT, who guard and cherish the Indian museum on the Hill and all that it represents.

Dedicated to

Randall Charles Zobel,
who walked a thousand miles.

This book was inspired by four men
of Good Medicine:

my father, **Richard Harold Fawcett,**
who inhales books and exhales their magic;
John Babcock Brown III / West Wind,
who hates books and encouraged
me to question their existence;
Joseph Bruchac, the good spirit
and great writer who provokes me;
and my great-uncle, **Chief Harold Tantaquidgeon,**
who taught me to honor the woodlands.

The Temple at Delphi
"FIRST, in this prayer, of all the gods I name
The prophet-mother Earth . . ."
    —Aeschylus (525–456 B.C.), *The Furies*

Mohegan Hill
"Close to the truth is as good as you'll ever get."
    —Catherine Lamphere, Mohegan Tribal Elder

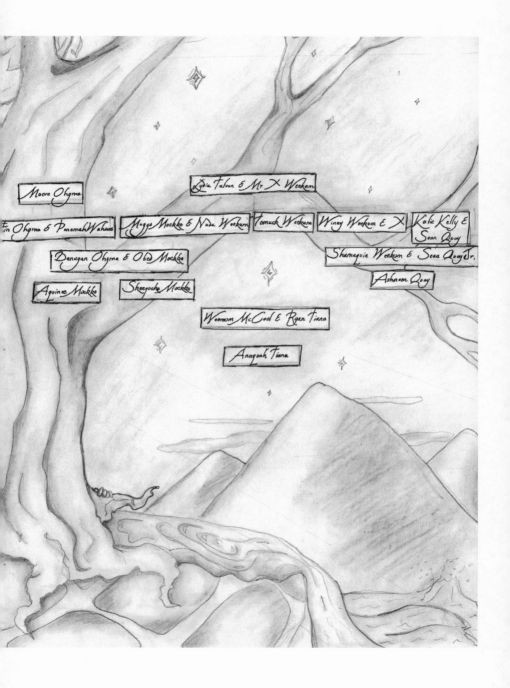

Maeve Ohgma

Lydia Faloon & Mr. X Weekam

Éin Ohgma & Ponemah Wahoue

Muggs Mockko & Nuda Weekam

Tomuck Weekam

Winay Weekum & X

Katie Kelly & Sean Qouy

Denugan Ohgma & Obed Mockke

Shamaquin Weekum & Sean Qouy Jr.

Agoince Mockko

Skeepucky Mockko

Ashneen Qouy

Weeroom McCool & Ryan Tiana

Anaqoah Tiana

CELESTIAL FAMILY
ANCIENT YANTUCK INDIAN STORY

At first, there was nothing at all. The Great Spirit was forever lost in space. Then, a fog extended across the nothingness and the Great Spirit brought forth the celestial family: the stars, our Grandfathers; the moon, our Grandmother; the sun, our Father; and the earth, our Mother; each formed in their own way to serve a special purpose.

Mother Earth was created atop the back of a giant turtle, also known to us as Grandfather. When the wind blew hard across Grandfather Turtle's back, the waters flowed off far and strong and the great mountains were born.

Father Sun shone down upon the

mountains of Mother Earth and brought forth the first tree, the Tree of Life. The Tree's limbs reached toward its father, the sun. But its roots remained forever connected to its mother, the earth.

As the Tree grew, it sent forth a shoot and that shoot became a man. Then the Tree bent over and touched Mother Earth to create the first woman.

Those first men and women were not as people are now. They were larger, louder, and even more cantankerous, for they lived in stormy times. But they had redeeming qualities: they fiercely protected their parents, the trees, and they lived in harmony with all of their relations, among the plant kingdom. These gigantic people were known as Beachers because they slept upon the sandy shores beside the sea. Their leader was the great Bawba, a man as colossal as the whales with whom he swam. His eyes were the color of the sea and his long hair floated about him like rippling seaweed.

After a time, the Age of Giants was no more, and Bawba and the Beachers were overrun by new, smaller people. The littlest among them held special magic, much like their Beacher forbears, and lived apart from the others. As the numbers of the new people grew, the Beachers were gradually called away by the winged beings to the Spirit World.

Many of the new

people forgot their Beacher ancestors. But from time to time, Bawba and his family crossed back over to visit those who kept their stories alive. Sometimes, they even bore children with them. Such children were often gifted with rare and ancient wisdom as well as prodigious size.

After the passing of the Beachers, many of the new people sensed that they were missing something. They sought prophets among those who still car-ried the ancient Beacher bloodlines. These prophets often lived high atop the world's greatest mountains, where they could touch both Mother Earth and Father Sky. People flocked to these lofty prophets with such intrusion that the Great Spirit chose to dis-

guise them as rocks. But ancient beings frequently gather at rocks, so they were shortly discovered and the Great Spirit then transformed them into trees.

However, when that disguise also failed, they were turned into stars, that they might shine safely, from afar. So it has been ever since. Earthly beings of great wisdom continue to twinkle throughout the oraios blackness of the universe.

CHAPTER 1
BLINK

Not So Many Moons From Now

The Indian casinos were now all gone.

The night the lights blinked out at Big Rock Casino, the stars returned to the evening sky. The children on the reservation huddled against anything familiar—all except little Ashneon Quay, who dove into the twinkling darkness like a luscious box of snowcap candies, licking her lips at the sugary dots sprinkled across the creamy chocolate night.

For most Yantuck Indians, Big Rock Casino down in Fire Hollow had been apex of their reservation. Its gleaming emerald spires leapt from the sandy riverbed in such a way that most could not resist calling it "Oz." Only a select few still believed that nearby Yantuck Mountain remained the true center of the universe. Of that loyal group, fewer still were chosen to become medicine people and serve as the mountain's sacred guardians. For the moment, ten-year-old Ashneon Quay was the youngest of those elite oracles, whose training and selection was the secret nub of all mountain activity.

Her turquoise eyes flashed as she zoomed toward the mountain summit, where there would be nothing between her and the glorious evening sky. She knew every jagged rock by heart; none bruised her feet, though they were protected only by the kind of buttery mocs that most Indians wore as house slippers.

From the mountaintop—only half a mile from that evening's

casino carnage—Ashneon Quay's view was sublime. She flopped blissfully onto a fuzzy mound of moss, confident that her great-uncle Tomuck and Grandma Winay would not be returning home to the Weekum House any time soon. Tonight, there were graver concerns than scolding children for being out alone late at night on the mountain.

Three thick chestnut braids spoked out from her head across the moss, like life ropes stretched upon an algae sea. As the moon slipped behind the puffy clouds, the girl drew a deep, lazy breath.

"Now it is truly night," she whispered.

Winay always said that the moon stole the life force when it vanished like that, but Ashneon had never felt more alive. Hooting owls and hissing bats whirled above her head, in search of fresh feast. She yearned to soar with them and beat her wings against the dusky sky.

From her velvety forest bed, Ashneon's eyes darted toward the shadowy box of the tribal museum. Her mind raced through the million and one lectures she had heard there, including Tomuck's most recent one.

"You need . . ." he had broken into his usual coughing jag, ". . . need water to balance your fire, girl."

"Like you need darkness to balance your light, right uncle?"

After growling out a phlegmy "hmmmrumph," he had limped away in surrender, each breath sounding more like a whistle.

This night, evening felt right for the first time. It was a glittering, black-beaded gala night, a night to celebrate and give thanks. Ashneon stretched heavenward toward the faraway flames that burnt up the mountain sky. The bright lights of Big Rock would never again ruin another evening for those masters of the night.

The glitzy casino down in the sandy hollow had never been further removed from the woodsy mountaintop. Before, Fire Hollow had circled its towering emerald gem with a golden glow like a shimmering crown, protecting its lofty pate from all outlanders. Now Fire Hollow appeared to be merely a colorless void beneath the mystical headland.

At the same moment Ashneon sprinted for the mountain peak, her great-uncle, Medicine Chief Tomuck Weekum, snatched a pistol barrel away from the CEO's head in Big Rock casino's back cash room. Meanwhile, her grandmother, Medicine Woman Winay Weekum, was coaxing down a mascara-smeared jumper from the ledge of the casino hotel's fifteenth floor.

In the weeks leading up to Big Rock's fateful shut-down, Chief Executive Officer Ryan Tianu had fired over two thousand Indians and only nine hundred and twenty-two others. Yes, all of his relatives were counting. For an Indian who was also a casino CEO, it was especially easy to forget what it meant to be tribal. Such forgetfulness had recently resulted in ever bolder remarks about Ryan's height. The casino warehouse guys regularly taunted him with lame repetitions of "How ya doin', big guy?" and the six A.M. employee aerobics class winked and cackled about the "Little Big Man." Then there was the tribal office staff, a ghoulish assemblage of third, fourth, and fifth cousins who regularly sniped around corners, with nicknames like *Sunjumeese* (Little Chief) and *Peegee* (Baby Wampum).

Ryan's ripely pregnant, russet-haired wife, Weeroum McCool Tianu, usually laughed off that sort of thing. After all, he was plenty man enough for all of her four feet six inches. But Ryan was not laughing at much these days. He had not told her about the recent anonymous threat to burn down the casino, addressed to Mr. Munchkin, slipped silently under his mahogany door.

The day before that threat was made good, Ryan sidled up to a dumpster with a bottle of Jameson whiskey slapped under his armpit and hollered up to Chief Tomuck Weekum's open office window.

"Sheef" he slurred, "I'm havin' a baby hull never see a sinel tribal stripen check."

A moment later, Tomuck's vein-crusted arm thrust out the window and released a rain of tobacco upon Ryan's head. "Your child is truly blessed," the Chief replied.

At that moment, Ryan could not imagine that those words were even close to the truth. There was no point in Tomuck trying to explain that the casino was, in fact, a false Messiah whose death heralded the fractious dawn of a legendary age: a time when the Yantuck would remember how to plant and how to fish, how to swim and how to fly; a time when the evening sky would no longer sizzle with a burning yellow glow—a truly magical time for a Yantuck child to be born.

Just before dawn, the dismantled carcass of Tomuck and Winay's brother-in-law, Muggs Mockko, joined the remains of several other tribal councilors on a screaming convoy to Thames Memorial Hospital. By daybreak, the spent paramedics needed their own stretchers. By noon, the slot machines had all been seized, the money impounded, and Beautiful Big Rock reduced to a sizzling bilious blob.

Winay staggered home around six A.M., the white knot of her hair caked with grease and blood. She was usually such a tight and tidy little medicine bundle that only the unimaginable could have left her like this. Before she had a chance to sit down, another set of all-American red, white, and blue flashes whizzed past her window. Upstairs, Ashneon had been snoring for hours when those sirens slapped her back to reality.

The child greeted the day in the only bedroom she had ever known. Winay had recently agreed to let her paint it luscious shades of "strawberries and cream." Through those windows, the day loomed even dimmer. The red fruitlet comforter crumpled under her chin for one last snug moment, before unfolding to the shattered dawn.

"Let's assess the damage," Winay instructed herself. As soon as she turned on the cy, the temperature spiked and the living room reeked of something unidentifiable. Someone had been fiddling with the controls again. Four out of five sense buttons were on and Tomuck tolerated a maximum of three. He and Winay were so old-fashioned, they might as well have just owned a television—were it not for the fact that the cy was an enemy whom they needed to keep close. By offering a virtual world of sight, sound, smell, taste and touch, the cy had mutated people's priorities. Kitties and puppies were worthless to children after even a brief romp with lions and hyenas on a cysafari, and all riots now included fire and odd-smelling smoke, simply to remain newsworthy.

. . . allegations of payoffs and cybates along with a recent push by tribal citizens to hike stipends and expand the tribal rolls in the face of rising debt contributed to the recent destabilization of the Yantuck tribal government and closure of Big Rock Casino. Following last night's suspicious fire, the President has called upon United Nations troops to restore order on the devastated east coast Indian reservation."

Winay could not pry her sticky eyelids fully open, but real sleep was out of the question. An incoming call on the cy jerked her back to the land of the living. Now she faced a split screen, with the President seducing voters with the latest market-tested aftershave on the left and her soot-soaked brother providing smouldering updates from ground zero on the right. Winay referred to such clashing cy emissions as crimes against the senses.

"Don't mind the smoke, Win," coughed Tomuck.

The eery viridian cloud that had been hovering above the hollow for the last hour now began to lean toward Yantuck Mountain. The minute Tomuck noticed crows exiting the mountaintop, he called in an advance warning to his sister—yet another signal to Winay that even at seventy-eight years of age, her brother remained a model Chief and, for the most part, a model human being. For the last six hours, he had battled murderous black jack dealers, championed the honor of cocktail waitresses, saved a few casino big-shots from themselves and slapped around members of his own Tribal Council. Now, he still remembered to call home a warning, out of policy. Always protect the home front. Tomuck was a true military man, through and through. Besides, he had certain other news that could not wait.

"Don't worry about the smoke headin' your way. Some genius decided to burn the whole place down," he continued. "But we got it all settled down now. Seems with sunrise comes sobriety."

"What about the latest wave of ambulances?" Her voice cracked on the last word.

"Oh that. Nothin' serious. Just some smoke inhalation is all . . . 'Cept . . ." He paused a split second too long. "It looks like ole Muggs didn't make it through the night. I just got word from the hospital."

"Oh, poor Nuda! I need to see our baby sister then, right away, sleep or no sleep."

Winay yanked up the blinds, cockeyed, to reveal Nuda and Muggs Mockko's immaculate front porch. A single, gray birch rocker stood at attention out front, ready to command the entire universe to share its grief.

"Tomuck, we gotta help her, no matter what kind of fool her husband was." The old woman turned up the volume with each successive phrase. "There's a piece of me that's never got over the mess he made, way back when. But that's all behind us, now. What worries me is how Muggs's death will affect the boy. I'm afraid Obed will . . ."

The old Chief cut off the crescendo with the pounding gavel of his black boot. "Sister, Obed has been a grown man for quite awhile now and he's got twins on the way any day. Our dear little sister spends enough time doting on him. Don't *you* start in now!"

Obed was the late Muggs and Nuda Mockko's only son. 'Til now, Tomuck and Winay Weekum had been able to dodge responsibility for their notorious nephew. After all, he took after Muggs's side of the family and was therefore Muggs's problem. But with Muggs gone, there was suddenly an unavoidable blight upon the Weekum family tree.

"Oh, Ashneon! Come here a minute, birdie!" squeaked Winay.

Her granddaughter's loose mocs slapped down the creaky stairs two at a time. The girl hit the ground running, even at the crack of dawn. What worried Winay was whether Ashneon was forever running *toward* her responsibilities, or *away* from them. Surely, there was no question about Ashneon's personal dedication to Winay and Tomuck; she would have fought right beside them that night if not for the recent minor's curfew on the reservation. But whether or not she would accept their decree to become the next Yantuck medicine woman—well, that was another story.

"Doesn't seem like you had any trouble sleeping," Winay muttered with her head down. She rarely faced Ashneon directly. The child's brilliant turquoise eyes had a hypnotic quality that sometimes forced even the old Medicine Woman to twitch in order to maintain minimal composure.

Winay pushed back the front door till its hinges moaned. It never swung fully open until after the first frost when her sea of clay pots, currently spilling a good eight feet into the yard, were hauled back indoors for the season. For now, balmy late-summer air permitted sweetgrass, old *nicotiana* tobacco, and other mysterious medicinals (known only to Winay) to block the doorway. Of course, the front door was the only part of the Weekum House exterior not fully choked with flora. Bittersweet, poison ivy, sumac, bull briars, lilacs, and beech sprouts ranged across its cedar shingles, allowing for only the occasionally peekable window. Inside, more pushy flora, both towering and tiny, commandeered each and every sunny nook.

"Well, how would *you* like to be pruned?" Winay snipped at anyone bold enough to question the leafy condition of her domicile. Winay was the Queen of Green.

"Let's step outside and have a look at this smoke your great-uncle warned us about. Whewee! Take a look at that! Here it comes. Bye, bye Big Rock," Winay squeezed her granddaughter's narrow ribs a bit too tightly amidst the potted jungle.

"Never forget this. Remember your people's capacity for foolishness, birdie."

"You knew this was coming, didn't you Win?" Ashneon folded her arms, "I know you can see the truth."

Winay dropped her snowy head, as if addressing the earth. "Well, maybe close to the truth. Medicine people don't see everything, you know. Only glimmers of what really is, what was, what is to come. Those glimmers help maintain the balance, and that is our only job."

Cowardly ghosts of smoke halted right before the pots, until a sudden southwest squall stormed the mountaintop, leaving Ashneon hacking and gagging on the toxic breeze.

"I have some bad news," Winay continued. It's about your great-uncle Muggs."

Her grandmother's words wended far away onto a shifting wind toward a place of smoke and fire within a memory long forgotten. And upon that wind and to the place, Ashneon followed . . .

The warm, thumping, mother's heartbeat had faded into silence. This first day in the world had been dreadful. The next proved no better. Long past dawn, the sky remained dim, as if the sun had not bothered rising. But for a flock of screeching crows, there was nothing to suggest that morning had broken. Sean Quay's gray pickup had blurred into the haze with enough foolish haste to send both newborn Ashneon and her father crashing into a valley of gold, blue, and amber flames. Now, Ashneon's father, too, was gone and fire surrounded the infant.

From deep within the flames, she could hear a woman's voice—not that of her mother—but a warm, deliciously liquid voice, nonetheless.

"Come Ashneon," it crooned, and the baby raised her pudgy arms toward the beckoning flames.

The voice continued, "If you want to see your mother, you must dance with me, within the flames!"

The baby's cheeks roasted to a lively crimson flush.

"Come now, dance with me and you will see your mother!" the silky voice prodded.

Suddenly, the baby's grandmother rushed in, scolding the flames, "No, you cannot have her, too."

Then, without warning, a great giant joined the group, immediately siding with the flames.

"The child does not want to go with you Medicine Woman! Let her join the fire! She craves the other side!"

But the grandmother snatched the baby away both from the giant and the alluring flames.

"Foolish Yantuck! You cannot save the girl from her destiny," the giant boomed. "Child, I will leave you to your grandmother, but know this," he stared, solidly, into baby Ashneon's deep turquoise

eyes, "Whenever you look into the mirror, you will be reminded that you are only one step away from the brightest fire and light of the universe. I cannot change that. You will forever be a part, not only of this world, but of the one beyond. You may visit the Spirit World at any time and when, one day, you pass over for your final, extended stay, you will still be called upon to aid the living. Two worlds shall forever be yours. That will be your gift and your curse!"

"Birdie! You all right?" Winay cradled the girl's head with a damp, red checkered dish towel.

"I'm fine, fine! Better than ever!" Blue-hot flares shot out from the girl's wide eyes as she slapped the sopping towel onto the kitchen floor and spun around, braids whirling like fringe on a grass dancer.

"Winay, listen, there is something weird about me and I know it has to do with my parents and the way I was born."

"Oh Birdie, your birth was tragic. Your mother hardly made it though your delivery. So much bleeding. I never . . ." The old woman's head began to wobble like a bobble-head toy, but she recovered. "I think your father was so distraught when he drove you home in that storm that, well, he just wasn't watching the road. Of course you don't remember that terrible accident down in the hollow. But you've seen quite a bit for such a young age. Haven't you?"

"That's just it Win, Now I—I remember the accident and other things too. The smoke, Uncle Muggs dying," she coughed. "It all reminded me of something, of someone."

"Aw dee baw ba," muttered Winay. "Birdie, I'm so sorry I can't bring you and your mother together again. I know that's your greatest wish."

"You don't need to be sorry anymore, Winay," Ashneon hrumphed, hands propped on non-existent hips, "I know now that, soon, I *will* visit my mother myself!"

CHAPTER 2

CORPORATE PROPHETS

Twelve Years Later

With Big Rock Casino long gone, no one cared about the Indian dregs who survived on Yantuck Mountain. Like all New England tribes, the Yantuck lacked silver jewelry, painted ponies, and grazing buffalo. They did not even have tipis and their pow wows sucked. They had fought the white man for so long, most of them were too beat-up to do anything but whine. The Yantuck were simply not tourist-ready.

Medicine Chief Tomuck Weekum was one of the few, crotchety oldtimers who still hung tough. He never whined, but he did bitch regularly about the antics of his people. His crooked fingers stroked the billowing bowl of his soapstone pipe as the surrounding atmosphere threatened to turn into a full-blown sweat lodge. There was powerful medicine in that old crop tobacco. Not only did it carry messages to the Spirit World, those who knew claimed it was like smoking velvet.

Right beside him, his sister vigorously belted out the Canoe Song—A Hey Ya Hey Ya Hey Ya Hey—positively reveling in the choking steam. After all, Winay was the reigning champion of the Emerald Kingdom, and on a planet teaming with would-be herbalists, that made her a shining star.

A funny thing, though, Winay hated any clothing or household accessory that carried even a hint of leafy green. "Dangerous and shameful mimicry," she called it. Most tribal members muttered privately about that notion, but no one dared challenge the Medicine Woman directly on the matter. There were far too many poisonous, allergic, and carnivorous plants in the world to take a chance on insulting the Queen of Green.

On the other hand, it could be argued that championing the Emerald Kingdom was an equally treacherous course. After all, insects viewed Winay as their arch-nemesis. Something as simple as an inspection of the backyard grape arbor prompted hundreds of Japanese beetles to flee her path like a storm of exploding shrapnel.

In an odd way, Winay's eccentric protegé, Ashneon Quay, was far more fortunate than the old lady. The young woman's habit of regularly visiting the Spirit World was clearly preferable to Winay's devotion to dying herbs. It is a time-honored fact that the dead are far less trouble than the dying.

The old Medicine Woman really had her hands full with the precarious livelihood of the plant creatures. Every day, she reverently set out gifts of whiskey and smokes for Bawba, the giant Beacher King who protected them. While most Yantuck did not believe in Bawba anymore (or in any of the legendary Beacher race, for that matter), few questioned Winay's devotional offerings. Her graphic descriptions of Bawba's gigantic white teeth, gleaming beneath yards of rippling seaweed locks, convinced all but the most arrogant to keep their mouths shut, just in case. While Ashneon remained one of only a few Indians who also believed in Bawba, she was in no way a fan and berated him as the mutant offspring of a beluga and a sequoia.

Unfortunately, each year's tributes to Bawba were increasingly abundant but less fruitful, which made Winay's goal of saving the Emerald Kingdom more and more elusive. Too little rain was followed by too much flooding. Searing heat waves were halted by blizzards. The weather had simply gone berserk and there was little that Bawba could do. He helped his green subjects as best he could. However, sometimes his methods were highly questionable.

Ashneon, on the other hand, never had much to do with the old lug. It was something of a turf war. She dodged Bawba whenever possible. But there was a limit to her success. Since many Indians take tree form in the afterlife, the cries of trees drew the attention of King Bawba, plant protector, and Ashneon Quay, spokeswoman for the dead. That made burial grounds a pretty dangerous place for Ashneon, except in fall and winter, for Bawba despised frost.

There was one time, though, when she was just thirteen, that Bawba challenged her, directly, on the matter of their concurrent travels to the Spirit World. Having just mastered the technique of visiting her mother on the other side, Ashneon had barely crossed over when she was greeted by Bawba's booming challenge: "Where do you think your power to travel between worlds comes from anyway, hmm mmm?" Before she could respond, he fluttered his great tree trunk arms above his head and wailed so loudly it nearly split her head open. Then poof, the monstrous old fellow was gone.

That hideous playground bully-chuckle was one of several personality features that encouraged Ashneon to remain scarce. It was the kind of laugh that made you feel alone and sur-rounded all at the same time. Besides, it was not as though Ashneon Quay appreciated being made to feel any more odd. Sure, other Medicine Women-In-Training spoke to their ances-tors in the Spirit World and some even made occasional trips to the other side, but no one except her regularly romped into the afterlife like they were dropping by the mall.

The need to achieve some degree of normalcy inspired her enrollment at Hoscott University. Of course, college presented its own set of conformity issues. Being raised on a sacred mountain-top by two Indian Medicine People made transitioning from the mountaintop to mid twenty-first century academia a more hel-lacious trip than passage between the living and the dead.

"College must be a breeze for you, birdie," Winay insisted. "Shouldn't interfere with any of the work we have to do around here!"

The Weekums truly believed their Indian Museum atop Yantuck Mountain was the center of the universe. Meanwhile, Dean Marion of the Hoscott College of Arts and Sciences disagreed. "If you want to get ahead and succeed here, young woman," she scolded, "your family needs to let you focus more on your books."

But there were so many books on the spring semester reading list and still such a mess of tribal documents to sort out at home. So little had been written down about the Yantuck Indians and now, presto, the world was banging down their door.

Today was another triple-digit day and everyone on the mountain had stripped down to the legal minimum—that is, all except Ashneon, who religiously wore her velvets topped off with miles of beads. That notorious attraction to beads inspired a longstanding tribal joke that Ashneon Quay was to blame for the original sale of Manhattan.

Final exam notes for Professor Peter Lymmel's "Indigenous Belief Systems 442" sat propped beside the griddle sputtering with oysters. The shellfish was courtesy of Tomuck's fans at YAQUA (Yantuck Aquaculture)—the last surviving tribal business. A brown sugar and honey glow radiated from the yellow-eyed beans, baking in the solar oven. All that was left to complete everyone's favorite Saturday night supper were the johnnycakes, their thick, sunny batter plopping off the sides of the maple wood mixing bowl.

Tomuck hobbled into the living room and let out a primal whoop, a sound that always made their hearts skip a beat. The folksy living room could have easily been mistaken for a New England antique shop were it not for the serious technology positioned at its nucleus. Ash splint baskets were piled high atop a roll top desk, flanked by frosted Victorian lamps and yellowing faunal and botanical prints. All seating, other than the high-tech cychair, consisted of hand-caned uprights with handmade afghans tossed across their dainty backs.

Tomuck's cychair was situated at the command center, fully equipped for five-sensory stimulation—even though only three "s" buttons (activating sight, sound, smell, and not taste or touch) currently glared in lime neon.

Tonight, Tomuck had dared to put on the news, in spite of his conviction that the cy was to television what the nuclear bomb was to dynamite. It was difficult to argue with that claim. Clearly, people were not meant to experience the full exhilaration of ax murders, pyroclastic flows, and terrorist bombings vaulting daily into their living room.

"You women come here a minute. You need to see this." Tomuck was circling his arms inward as though beckoning the forces of nature.

The cy spewed forth the news in brilliant sight, sound and smell, "The Oracles take on NASA and all prophecies are good! Good Evening, I'm Rain Sky Wu. Welcome to CBN, Cybusiness News, New Light Edition . . ."

A glamorous Asian cycaster wore a gold and amber necklace embossed with a smiling sun. The tips of her pencil-straight hair had been dipped in complimentary Gold Luster, lending her an irresistible, Cleopatra-like quality.

"More about this and other stories when we return," the golden beauty concluded.

"Jesus. Oh Jesus!" shouted Tomuck. "Whoop, Whoop! You women get in here!"

The old Chief had edged his rickety frame so far off the cychair, it was difficult to say exactly what was holding him up.

"What? What! Are you OK?" asked Ashneon, rocketing into the room without making a sound. That whist velocity had prompted some to claim that Ashneon could materialize out of thin air. Closer to the truth was the fact that she sprang about like a neurotic young mother because she forever imagined terrible harm coming to the two fragile beings entrusted in her care. That fear was surpassed only by a paralyzing angst over her own destiny once they were gone.

"Here. Sit right here and watch this," he ordered her into one of the caned chairs. "This is where your cousin Obed Mockko's foolishness is going."

"What are you yelling at her for?" Winay muscled in, shoving a wayward snowy tendril back into a perfect bun. Today there was a biting, golden glint in Winay's eyes, a sign her family knew only too well.

Tomuck backed off. "Ain't nobody yelling at nobody. Jesus Win, just sit down and listen to the cy. That ol' rainy day china woman will be back in a minute. There now, here we go!"

Winay remained standing, defiantly affording the seat to the bowl of johnnycake batter. Having concluded a series of vanilla-laden commercial interruptions, the cy shifted to a rose petal-scented station identification, followed by an exotic whiff of spicy Middle Eastern potpourri, signaling the onset of the main event.

"Today on Wall Street, the Vatican dropped seven-eighths of a point as shares in New Light Corporation skyrocketed following news that New Light has secured exclusive broadcast rights for Delphi I, the world's first spiritual space station. We turn now to Proudfoot Levine, live from New Light headquarters in Sotona. Proudfoot?"

Patchouli and frankincense wafted into the room, destined to clash mightily with the New English salt pond oysters and baked beans.

"Good Evening, Rain Sky. This is Sotona, home base for a small group of spiritual seekers who call themselves New

Lighters. These men and women have spent years looking to introduce the online world to a consortium of the world's greatest avatars, popularly known as the Oracles. Now, with the advent of Delphi I, the world's first spiritual space station, New Light shamanic blue chips are expected to make an unprecedented surge. These avatars among the stars will only be accessible to those willing to pay the blockbuster admission fee."

"Oracles! Well, that's enough of that," said Tomuck switching the cy station.

"Wait, Uncle, this is important. You put it on. Remember?" pleaded Ashneon.

"AACH foolishness. Nuf!" He was wheezing again.

Tomuck switched to the Hubble channel, settling back to curse the latest insanity from Mars.

"Fine, Uncle, fine. Can you believe that cy?"Ashneon whipped toward Winay.

"Don't know any better, I suppose, birdie," Winay shrugged and threw a towel over the johnnycake batter. "Your cousin Obed has been hooked up with those New Lighters for quite a while now. I'll bet he's in on all this oracle business. He is into some big money this time."

"Cousin Obed." Ashneon pointed as though reading a marquis, "The Man With All The Medicine In The World But Who Squanders It On Fools."

"You and he were always oil to vinegar. I'm calling my sister on this one," said Winay.

"You know *she's* watching the New Light news," snapped Ashneon.

"Aquay, Sister," said Winay "My, you're looking kind of peaked. Were you watching the New Light news?"

"Oh, please," groaned Ashneon. Her late mother, Shamaquin, had repeatedly warned her about Nuda.

"Yes, yes, Nuda, that's just your favorite grandniece," said

Winay. "She's been anxious about knowing what all this mess has to do with your son . . . Oh, so Obed'll be calling you tonight," Winay grumbled.

Ashneon mouthed the words, "Big surprise," then screamed, "save!" at the slightly deaf old cyscreen. "Listen to this, my dear Oracles-to-be," she turned to face Tomuck and Winay, "New Light Corporation to feature Hidden Oracles of Native America for the start of the fiscal year, October first. I'll bet that's your debut date. Dear cousin Obed has surely sent in your résumés." She scowled at the phone. "He'd better not expect you two to blast off anywhere!"

Winay shooed Ashneon to hush. "See you at dinner tomorrow, Sister."

"Anyhow, doesn't he remember how we lost the casino?" Ashneon maintained an uzi pace and a tone just a hair below yelling, "I am two decades younger than Obed and I remember the filthy mess." A subtle shift in eye color, from turquoise to teal, was always detectable at times like these.

"Ashneon, when Indians walk away from the Creator and start running toward the dollar, it's much worse than for other folks," preached Winay. "But, when our very own medicine family starts running there . . ."

Whatever reservations the Yantuck had about the old Medicine Woman's peculiar relationship with plants and giants, everyone knew that when it came to tribal business Winay Weekum perched "center on the beam." Her voice never rose up too high or fell down too low—at least most of the time. Her brother, Tomuck, on the other hand, regularly wound up tight and sprung loose over the least little thing—just like Ashneon. Both of them burned in short, meteoric bursts, like falling stars.

The old man dove in, "Greed, greed, greed. Every one of those God-damned fools thought we were stealing their money, back in them casino days. I'll tell you what really happened: they figured being Indian was outdated. Claimed they were going to have an American democracy and vote on everything. Trouble was, them idiots wanted a popular vote! Ha! You notice them Americans are too smart to let democracy foul up their corporate businesses. That tribal trash wanted something to say about every expenditure we made at that casino. The word of the Medicine Chief didn't mean nothin' to 'em. Didn't want to hear about the future I predicted for 'em if they kept on holdin' things up. Well they got what they wanted. Brought everything to a screeching halt."

Thin, shredded bits of air whistled between Tomuck's teeth as he hopped up and down, but he was not about to stop.

"So, here we are, has-been operators of one of the last and best casinos ever was. Busted. And not because of the white man. No, can't blame him for much this time. Only ones truly to blame are ourselves. Damn fool Indians going right back into the pit with the copperheads again."

After Tomuck tightened his belt to its final notch, Winay slunk away, hopeful of avoiding both her brother's tirade and the painful reality of his ever-shrinking form.

The scrawny old man resumed his peppery dance, bobbing back and forth, and up and down at the same time. How his stringy, gray ponytail remained forever corralled in its trusty leather tie remained an eternal mystery.

He continued to address Ashneon while backhandedly shooing Winay's retreating form. "Mind you, that casino crash did have a windfall. All them fair-weather Indians blew away like dandelion fluff! But people forget, and now we're headed on down the same trail. Won't get out of it this time. Nope. Now even the Indians are selling their religion, or better yet, their religious leaders. Gonna shoot their Medicine People off into space, in fact! I don't envy you the task ahead, girl. White man taught 'em well is all I have to say."

Tomuck dropped like a feather onto the arm of his cychair for the blue-lipped finale. "Anyway, sad truth is, the white man's smarter than the Indian now. Even he's figured out that money ain't all there is to life. That rainwoman on the cy was half right. These days, white man actually is seeking a new light, looking for his lost spirit or soul—or whatever he calls it this week. Meanwhile, the Indian is saying, 'I never lost my spirit, so now that you've lost yours, why don't you come and take mine. It won't cost too much.' And white man, what does he say? 'Don't mind if I do!'"

CHAPTER 3

MESSAGES

"Tomuck smoothed back his long, silver threads to reveal the shadowy caverns of his cheeks. Looking Nuda's two grandchildren in the eye, he frowned. "You two still taking those instrument lessons?"

"You know we are, Uncle," said Aquinnee. She was eleven, a full year older than her brother, Skeezucks, and therefore entitled to answer for them both.

"We have our Spring recital coming up this week, Uncle!" Skeezucks lit up for a second, then fizzled, like a dud firecracker.

Who cared that he was performing. His sister was the darling of the local cymusic community but Skeezucks's archaic flute sounds were blackballed by that crowd.

"Well you look for me in the front row. I'll be there," Tomuck assured.

As Skeezucks struggled to remember the last time Tomuck had actually set foot off Yantuck Mountain, his chin crumpled atop his wrist. On the other hand, Tomuck did have certain abilities that were not quite human, so it was conceivable that he could find a way to hear the recital and whittle on the mountain simultaneously.

"Aquinnee, you go ahead and say grace," authorized Winay.

A cascade of raven hair tumbled down the girl's back and onto the seat as the child launched her sharp chin toward the sun.

"*Tawbut ni tukenig kah weous. Niyayomo.*"

"Thank you Aquinnee. And who taught you to hold your head up that way when you pray, I wonder?" inquired Tomuck, wrinkling his brow into a series of worn-out trails.

"Ashneon says we should pray the old way, addressing

Father Sun. That way he can hear our messages clearly. She says Amen really refers to the Egyptian Sun God, Amen Ra, and that the Christians didn't know that's what they were saying."

Tomuck hissed between his remaining front teeth, "I see. And I suppose your cousin, Ashneon, knows all that because she's spoken to old-time dead folk, again, and asked them how they did things." He waggled a cadaverous finger at his two grand-nieces.

Even Tomuck had a hard time with Ashneon's claims of regular rendezvous with the dead. Outside of the Weekum family, Ashneon was viewed as a fully delusional young woman who had fabricated afterlife journeys as an artificial coping mechanism to deal with the deaths of her parents.

"Actually . . ." Ashneon defended.

Winay broke in, "Oh no, you two, that's enough of that. Not dinner talk."

"Win, you're the one who chose this here bookish beauty to follow in your footsteps and the little one's cut from the same cloth," Tomuck chided. "Two peas in a pod."

Aquinnee sat as tall as she could. Few women merited comparison to Ashneon Quay. Though you could not truly call Ashneon beautiful. Entrancing, perhaps, but never beautiful. It had something to do with the fact that she defied the standard tableau. She simply had too much chestnut hair, eyes that were far too bright, a shrunken frame that was clearly too compact, and riveting facial expressions that often went well beyond severe. Of course, when you came right down to it, it was those turquoise eyes that had made her a living legend.

Rumor had it that her mother, Shamaquin, had gasped at the sight of those eyes the moment she died. To Ashneon, that meant her eyes were nothing more than a wicked curse, a blazing blue reminder of a newborn Indian, somehow painted wrong.

It was true. Ashneon had been cursed, but why and how was known only to the chosen few. When she was a little girl, Ashneon heard two old women down in the hollow saying that those wicked eyes came from a father who was that kind of Indian, the type who had so little Native blood, he could be tossed off the tribal rolls if he nicked himself shaving.

Of course Fire Hollow gave rise to many stupid rumors. The ka-ching of lively slot bells had been replaced with the rancid echoes of dull footsteps. The worst tribal stragglers wandered through that mangy ghost town. Eating too little and drinking too much, they blamed their troubles on everyone but themselves. Over the last decade those burrowing maggots had stripped Beautiful Big Rock right down to her rebar bones.

Ashneon kept her little cousins, Aquinnee and Skeezucks, well away from Fire Hollow. They were her children now and maybe forever. Shortly before dying, their late mother, Danugun, had enlisted Ashneon to train them in the ancient way. Ashneon decided that meant isolating them from all tribal trash, especially the foul variety that lurked in the hollow.

"Is Tashteh bringing by any amber mushrooms this week? It's been wet enough." Sheezucks poked Ashneon's upper arm.

Tashteh Sook may have been from another tribe but he was the kind of father that Skeezucks truly deserved. He had trained Skeezucks well: taught him that those amber mushrooms were ancient beings only to be eaten when the proper thanks was offered and that consuming them meant ingesting the essence of a tree, which was an earned thing.

The boy never took off the eagle talon necklace Tashteh had given him. Even though Tashteh's tribal stomping grounds were on the opposite side of the Quinnepaug River, Skeezucks knew that real Medicine People were the same everywhere. Ashneon knew it too. She and Tashteh had shared unspoken volumes since childhood.

Still, Skeezucks's own wayward father, Obed, had been the very best mushroomer as a young man, retaining a keen mental map of every proven oak stump on the mountain. Of course, he had not mushroomed, or even visited the mountain much since his wife, Danugun, died. Now rumor had it he was coming back and the mountain was ablaze with watch fires.

Nuda cleared her throat with a wet gurgle as though dislodging clogged plumbing, then dumped out the foul contents. "The children's father mentioned an upcoming visit."

Aquinnee's glass toppled, flinging a crystal pool across the table that dribbled directly onto Skeezucks's lap.

"Not again! Every time!" Skeezucks growled cantankerously.

"Time for your Grandma Nuda to get ready to perform the tea leaf reading!"

Ashneon excused the children from the table and whisked away their still-full bowls. They never did like succotash much, even though it was her favorite. A tray of pineo and mushroom sandwiches would perk them up. She cut the crust off their bread and dropped it into a basket for the birds. A crow whistled past the window, its mouth stuffed with the dried corn she had left out yesterday. No matter how fast she moved, Ashneon could not compete with the birds, soaring through the air, becoming the wind.

Winay was the one who taught her to watch the winged beings:

Remember: birds are very old creatures with an ancient purpose. They bring messages to and from the Spirit World.

Ashneon knew that she and the birds shared the same purpose in life.

✦ ✦ ✦

Ashneon joked that the tea leaves spoke to Nuda because her real father was King Bawba, gaint-guardian of the plant kingdom. Winay never found that funny. Still, Nuda had once cleared six feet (before she began to slump). And as if that was not suspect enough, there was also the talk about her hair.

The oldtimers swore that Nuda had hacked off a full three feet of gorgeous, flowing waves the day her husband Muggs died. After that, they said her hair never grew back one single inch, remaining forever bobbed about her chin, never quite reaching her neck and suspiciously devoid of gray at eighty years of age. Winay insisted that all that talk was just foolishness. Nuda probably just snuck off to some Garden City salon when no one was looking.

The most controversial aspect of Nuda Mockko was her restriction of her tea leaf readings to Indian women only. In a world where fortune-tellers sold out to the highest bidder, Nuda Mockko maintained her principles. Still, Ashneon was not sure if Nuda imposed that contentious rule by choice or out of some quirky necessity. Either way the truth about the restriction was locked in the Fort Knox of Nuda's mind.

"So who's going first today?" hollered Nuda from the dining room.

"Can I?" gasped Aquinnee, surveying the room for approval.

No fortunes were read to anyone under eleven; but Aquinnee had turned eleven one month ago and was feeling exceedingly privileged.

"Ashneon," mumbled Aquinnee, stuffing her mouth full of mushroom sandwich. "Everything she told me last week came true. All of it! There was the part about you teaching me that cleansing ceremony and that Dad was going to call!"

Skeezucks rolled his eyes, kicked a chair leg, snatched a sandwich, and flew out the door.

"Aquinnee, you think my fortunes are all true, eh? They're really only 'close to the truth,'" insisted Nuda.

"Close to the truth is as as good as you'll ever get," Winay chimed in.

The fortune-teller tossed back a mighty slug of her odd-looking tea and smacked her lips.

Tea leaf readings always transformed the dining room. Lights were shut off and replaced with antique oil lamps. Today, Nuda's "extras" included an iridescent sapphire tablecloth flecked with stars, moons, and marbled earthlets that winked beneath the lamplight, framing each fortune with a glittering cosmic storm.

Ashneon believed this setup was a ridiculous affectation, inspired only by Nuda's inability to resist shopping at the Wiccan booths at each and every New Light psychic fair.

Outside, Tomuck demonstrated the fine art of whittling to his grand-nephew—shaving gossamer layers off a maple log—while Skeezucks mind-melded with his new Shapeshifter game.

The old man snorted at the sign on the path leading to the museum, which read, "Observe, concentrate, remember."

"I know, really," said Skeezucks. "I'm almost finished. I promise."

A great southwest wind rattled the window panes as Ashneon and Winay hunkered down beside the kitchen table. It was a blustery, turkey vulture day, with those blood-faced buzzards circling in ever-widening rings just about everywhere. The trees were in transition from bud red to mint green and a thick, drippy fog oozed over the mountain. Lichen poked out from the mist like seafoam polka dots on the rocks and trees. Every few minutes, another gust rocked the windows.

Winay whispered to Ashneon, "You know it's time I had Aquinnee help me encourage some of the new spring shoots."

A moment later, they overheard Nuda saying, "You have a

bright and starry-eyed future young lady, but that means you're about to assume more responsibilities that may limit your fun time."

"Always on it, isn't she?" confirmed Winay.

Ashneon yanked the crystal doorknob shut. Fortunes were supposed to be private.

"Whoop!" shouted Nuda. "Next!"

In spite of her aversion to New Light practitioners, Ashneon knew there was no one better equipped to read the leaves than Nuda Weekum Mockko. Trembling across the threshold, she slurped down the remaining drops. A quick tip ensured that no leaves remained at he bottom or on the rim—a time-honored safeguard designed to protect against lost treasures. The three turns for good luck before handing over the fateful vessel. That was the custom.

Nuda's eyes fixed upon one tall stringy leaf, near, but not quite at, the cup's rosebud-trimmed rim.

"You'll soon be getting an insight about your research which is exactly what you've been waiting for, but not at all what you expect."

Probing a bit lower, the fortune-teller sang out, "Ooh my, there's a man in your life and it's seee-rious!"

"Is it Peter?" Ashneon gasped, edging closer to the cup for any perceptible clues.

Nuda flinched as the china roses whirled before her eyes, framing some clearly shocking future event. Ashneon's stomach soured.

"Oh nothing to worry about, Ashneon. Just says your greatest wish will be fulfilled. Guess we can't want for more than that, now can we?"

Nuda began to nestle into her chair, an action that always preceded an uncomfortable topic. She sighed, "I only wish I could hear from Muggs again. He ever speak to you on your trips to the other side?"

Ashneon shook her head no.

"No, I suppose not." The fortune teller's eyes glazed over as she slurped her barren teacup.

Muggs was only one of many mystery men of Yantuck Mountain.

Winay's husband was pure fable. Tribal legend had it that they met while she was away on tribal business. Once Winay almost said his name then tromped outside to shower expletives upon an unsuspecting willow tree.

It was nearly as bad with Winay's own mother, Priddie Liddie, the famed beauty. At least in the case of her mysterious husband, the Weekum surname survived, making it theoretically possible to perform an online DNA trace of the three Weekum children: Winay, Tomuck, and Nuda. But all the data showed was that Mr. Weekum was from Cape Cod, Massachusetts.

Surviving tribal folklore claimed that Priddie Liddie and her enigmatic mate had lived in an isolated lighthouse off Holler Beach until the locals discovered something unspeakable, something bad enough to have forced great-grandma Liddie and her brood out of town, minus Mr. Weekum, in a hurry.

But what could have possibly been considered unspeakable on the eastern seaboard by the early twentieth century?

Perhaps the tales of the Squanneeset Indians carried a grain of truth. They said Holler Beach was named for a tiny woman who became the unwitting mate of one of the giant Beachers. According to the tale, a Beacher transformed her human husband into a tree, then left her alone, bereaved, pregnant, and "hollering" beside the sea. The tribe said the Beachers made a habit of roaming the coasts of the world, emerging occasionally from the fog to unite with those who carried the blood of the Little People in order to maintain balance for Mother Earth.

But of course that is only a legend.

"Hey, Skeezucks!" yelled Ashneon. "How about getting some birch branches so I can fix us a pitcher of birch water for later?"

"Sure, Ashneon." The boy spun away from his electronic snare.

Skeezucks's hair streamed behind him like shiny black satin ribbons as he bolted up the path. Tomuck offered his grandniece a grateful navy salute. Skeezucks had better things to do than play with cygames. Some said his fleet-footedness came from years of wooshing up and down Yantuck Mountain with those mile-high legs.

Tomuck disagreed. "The boy flies like the crow on the great southwest wind."

Like Ashneon, Skeezucks used his hair as a distraction from his eyes, which were an eerie seaweed color imported from the Emerald Isle by his grandfather, Fin Ohgma. Like his grandfather and mother, Skeezucks's Irish eyes both damned and empowered his gaze.

After trotting back down the mountain, Skeezucks pumped both eyebrows up and down and winked at Ashneon, "I bet Tashteh will want some of this birch water. Want me to put some aside for him?"

Ashneon scowled and drummed her fingers on her hips. But it was too late. Brilliant strawberry patches had begun to flare up on her cheeks. Tomuck caught on immediately. Ashneon knew that Tomuck and her mother, Shamaquin, shared both a love for Tashteh and a powerful disdain for Dr. Peter Lymmel, the ponytailed professor.

The old man shook his head. "Now take Tashteh Sook. He may not be from your side of the river, but that man carries some mighty medicine. A far cry from that bookish weakling you want to marry, Medicine Girl. You and Tashteh been walkin' the same path forever. That's a mighty thing. Whole lot different than you and ol' Lyman. You and him don't even see the same path when you're walkin' it side by side."

The old man snickered at Peter's textbook, flipping its sheer flimsy pages, before finally letting it flop onto the floor with a limp, dull thud.

Ashneon scowled. "For the record, I haven't given much thought to marrying either Peter or Tashteh. I'm only twenty-two, remember. Besides, Tashteh is just a good friend and Peter is not a bookish weakling."

"You're nearly twenty-three," Tomuck corrected. "So, of course you may do what you want. But your friend Tashteh don't see the white man's world, and that Doctor Lyman, he don't see the Indian world."

"Lymmel," corrected Ashneon.

"Same difference," blurted Tomuck. "But remember, girl: it's Spring. So if you do make up your mind to marry some blind man, just be sure to pick the one who's blind to what don't matter to you. Real Medicine People are the same everywhere. Just you remember that."

Tomuck's eyes gleamed like polished obsidian, thus reminding Ashneon that his looks had once been the stuff of legend. Top modeling agencies once offered obscene contracts to claim that chiseled face and physique, but none were signed. Now the would-be cover boy was no more than a whiff of aftershave beneath a cowboy hat. His arthritis no longer responded to Winay's mullein and grape leaf wraps. Her disclaimer was that pollution had so altered the plants they could no longer be expected to do their job.

The old Chief's physical strain was compounded by the agony of watching his people fail. Many men coveted his title of Medicine Chief, but none was up to the challenge.

"Ashneon, some folks from Bolderton were up at the museum the other day, going on about that Oracle business. I told them that's got nothing to do with me."

"Since you brought it up, down at the hollow the other day, those fools down the tribal office were saying that since all our other economic developments have failed, you and Winay should sell your spiritual gifts and become Oracles for New Light Corporation."

"All foolishness. We're nothin' but a link in a great chain."

"That, my dear uncle, is just the kind of profound statement that makes all of your relatives think of you as pure avatar gold."

"So, our medicine used to be safe here. But now them Oracle fools are comin' 'round the mountain." He continued, "Ashneon, you remember what I taught you about that stone mortar and pestle up at the Longhouse?"

"Yes, of course." She droned, "You said that a mortar and pestle are the very symbols of life; that an Indian woman cannot do without them and that an Indian man must make them for her. You also said that to make a mortar, you must turn a stone with a hole big enough to hold water."

"You got it, Medicine Girl, that's where we're at. Obed's been up to his tricks for years. It's just that today's the day we discovered he has finished making his hole."

+ ✦ +

ORACLES
AN ANCIENT GREEK STORY

Near Dodona, there once stood an enormous oak tree with an extraordinary black bird nested in it. Many people visited there to observe the rustling of the tree and the flapping of the black bird's wings. Their movements were viewed as omens and the Greeks referred to the tree and the bird as their Oracles. For many years, the Oracles wisely guided and protected the flora and fauna of Dodona, including the human beings. As time passed, new Oracles appeared in Dodona and throughout Greece. These new prophets were neither plants nor animals, but human beings. Soon, the people forgot to listen to the birds and the trees. They came to believe that all plants and animals had been created to serve them. Thus, the birds and trees were ultimately disregarded as prophets.

That was the beginning of a dangerous time . . .

CHAPTER 4
BOOKS

Peter was rapping smartly on the door.

Why couldn't Tashteh love books, like Peter?

Peter had everything—minus those qualities Ashneon could respect in a man.

"Hello, Ashneon. Been up all morning with the birds again?"

Despite the blazing sun, the lofty professor was bedecked in colorless woolies from the local Goodwill. Long ago, colleagues had instructed him to dress down to the Natives, wear plain clothes so as not to offend. Obviously none of them had ever attended a Pow Wow.

"How do you visit with your friends on the cy, when your waking moments are so vastly different from the rest of the world?" he asked.

"Believe it or not, I still have one or two friends who don't depend on the cy to maintain our relationship," she snipped.

"And who might they be?" he chuckled. "Mr. Tashteh Sook, I presume?" The question droned from his lips in a pseudo-British accent, like he was suffering a colonialist spasm.

Settled atop a worn velvet pillow on the polished hickory floor, Ashneon kept right on sorting papers. The subject of Tashteh Sook was off-limits and not open to anthropological review. Anyway, Tashteh was just a friend. He did not inspire breathless moments, like Peter. With Tashteh, it was just the opposite. He allowed Ashneon to breathe slower and more deeply.

Peter and Ashneon's research pile had grown into three unstable towers, dividing all tribal records into BC, DC, and AC—before, during and after the Tribe's casino.

"Hey, you finally got some more of this stuff into the database! I thought I owned this mess," he said.

Peter's lips shone glossy red from sucking on a cherry lollipop.

"You haven't exactly been much help, lately, for such a scholarly woman." Leaning forward, he scolded her with the lollipop. "It's all right. Even if you forsake the quest, I will never leave you. Didn't one of your great Chiefs say, 'I will never leave you'? Anyway you know it's true. I'll hound you forever." He snagged her retreating arm.

"They say white men are fond of making promises they can't keep," she folded her arms.

"Ouch! I guess we earned that one."

Peter wriggled his hand back inside his pocket, sprouting a mountainous bicep.

Ashneon gulped. "Want a cold fruit drink? What is it, 110 degrees out there?"

"Anything BUT that cranberry of yours," he insisted, jabbing her rib with his elbow.

"I know you're an apple man," she sneered.

A smooth, flannel coziness set in as the research partners sipped fruit juice, huddled together on the floor. No need to worry, every time her heart began to flutter, her breathing became shallow, or her palms went clammy, some tribal crisis broke the spell. After all, Tashteh and Tomuck would not much like it if they thought their Medicine Girl was captivated by some incidental (Tomuck's pet term for anyone who lived beyond the mountain).

Still, there was something about those long, lean tendons at the back of Peter's neck when he bent over books. She wiped her slippery hands on her skirt.

"Maybe we should go over those old language mimeos that we found the other day," he suggested, slurping one last, noisy bit of juice. "Of course, you're the boss."

"Why am I not convinced of that fact?" Ashneon squinted her turquoise eyes. "Isn't that what they teach you white ethnographers: 'be submissive and you won't overwhelm the primitive folk, or . . . '"

"What do you think this is, Ashneon, the twentieth century?" he cut in. "On a more important note, I heard about ol' New Light Corporation and the Oracles. My cy's been beeping off the hook with inquiries about your tribe."

The room went blurry for a moment as Shamaquin flashed by. That was mother's standard invitation to please drop by, as soon as possible, for an important chat. Of course, Shamaquin found any excuse to break up a day with Peter.

"Whoa. Excuse me, Peter, what did you say?" Ashneon recovered. "You be sure to direct any cyporters to the tribal office or to me. Don't take the liberty of answering for us!"

Those idiots at the tribal office were, after all, kindred idiots, and he had no right to overstep them. Peter's neck was not really so lean at all. It was stringy, actually, and quite as limp as a hanging Peking duck. He was a pathetic excuse for a man with granola sandals, a flat ass, and a crushed chest. Besides, he crossed his legs like a woman.

"Hey, I hear you. You're the boss. I know my place. I'm just the hired hand anthropology boy."

He hopped on top of a beat-up Oxford English Dictionary and flung his arms open wide, declaring, "I'm just a scientist looking for the facts."

He was sadly adorable.

She sighed, "O great scientist, how was London last night? Damp? Dreary? Her eyebrow cocked sharply. "You did go on the cy yesterday for that meeting with the Brits?"

Peter bit his lip. "Yup. Surprised, aren't you. The head research guy reeked of mildewed sheep. Glad I wasn't actually there." Peter cleared is throat and continued, "to answer your question: that stone pendant of Winay's is over fifty thousand years old. You were right."

The findings remained tightly clenched in his hairy, freckled fist.

She ground her molars together. "I wasn't the one who needed confirmation. And frankly, I'm surprised you weren't too busy butting into our Yantuck tribal business to have the time to find out." Ashneon lunged over his lap. "Let me see what the Brits put out."

Peter drew back just enough to require a truly precarious dip. A tiny foot slipped, then a knee, plunging her bottomward into the trap. A beaded wrist caught hold of the chair in the nick of time, affording a relatively clean escape, considering.

"You all right?" he pouted. "You know you're not the only one worried about when these New Light corporate jerks will show up. They scrounged a United Nations Charter, you know. That means Winay's records may come under I-FOR-I, that New Light law for 'international freedom of religious information' bullshit. You don't suppose tribal police or the Tribal Council can do something to hold them off if the UN shows up looking for these papers?"

"That's pretty funny," she said. "Remember, these so-called Indians think Winay and Tomuck are their tickets to New Light cash. And the tribal cops just seem fierce to you because they would never wear sandals and they eat meat. And let's see, UN forces are mainly British and French. So, let's consider our tribal track record in opposing those folks at anything!"

Peter threw a pen at her. "Never mind. It will all work out. Tomuck and Winay Weekum's world lives on through you. You're the best one to write about them and record their knowledge. And everybody says you're the next one in line to take over their responsibilities."

"Everyone except me!" she fired. "Don't you think I would

know that if it were true? And didn't we agree you wouldn't bring that subject up if we were going to work together?"

"Sorry Ashneon, but they did train you," he twitched his nose smugly.

"All I know is that I just don't feel like the chosen one and none of the folks that I talk to on the other side have mentioned anything about me . . ."

"Whoa, whoa, whoa, what folks on the other side?" he interrupted, gripping her shoulders. "I thought you had let up on that heavy channeling stuff."

Ashneon shook Peter off, leaving his hands suspended in mid air.

The room was beginning to shrink-wrap around him.

Shelves covered with brittle baskets and yellowed photos of ancestors appeared to sally forth like infantry. The occupants of the Weekum House were circling the wagons.

"For the zillionth time, I do not channel, neither do I astral project, nor teleport," she explained. "When I cross over to the Spirit World, I merely travel through an organic portal. Then, I talk to certain people on the other side. It's almost as simple as when you go for a walk. Unfortunately, I am limited. There are some things I cannot ask them. But one thing is for sure: no one over there has ever mentioned anything about me becoming a Medicine Woman, Oracle, or whatever."

He began to open his mouth but she cut him off. "And no, you cannot observe me embarking on my journey and take field notes."

"But Ashneon, like you said, the people on the other side may just not happen to mention certain subjects. Anyway, I wish you would stop doing that traveling, tripping, or whatever it is that you do. It's morbid and it seems really dangerous. I understand about wanting to visit with your dead mother and all, but the whole thing is—well, unnatural."

"Unnatural!" she shouted. "This judgment from the man whose people have cloned the wooly mammoth! Forcing the dead back into this realm! You think that's natural?"

She drew a deep breath and burst out again, "Regardless of your opinion, Peter Lymmel, I will visit my dead mother. But I won't bring her back with me! If she was locked away in some gloomy white nut house or convalescent home, you would think it perfectly natural that I go and spend time with her. But just because she has no earthly form does not mean I have forsaken her. Oh, and she's not crazy about you, either, by the way. That she has told me."

Peter knew better than to dip his oar in again.

"Oh yeah, I almost forgot," she continued. "Winay wanted us to look over some of her old writings on projects. I glanced through them already."

"Projects? What kind of projects are you talking about? Home improvement?" quipped Peter.

"Say you're kidding. You've been working with me since when? Projects are the 'Injun' word for spells—you know, in-ca-han-tay-shee-ons!" she flitted her conjuring fingers up and down.

"You are kidding about not knowing that. Right, Peter?"

He crossed his heart. "Nope, not kidding. But I do know not to mess with them. It's not recommended."

She thrust a spiral binder across the tabletop. "You'll love 'em, she said. "No white man has ever seen these before." The corners of her mouth twirled up into a grinchly expression that in no way resembled a smile.

"I have an errand to run." She rocketed past him to meet her mother. "Someone needs to see me right away. I'll be back in an hour. Enjoy yourself!"

Peter lunged for the binder with all the hesitation of an addict greeting a tardy fix.

✦ ✦ ✦

Shamaquin Weekum Quay had been buried beneath a thigh-high boulder with a bronze plaque screwed to the front. Not just any boulder, but the one she had loved to jump off into the Quinnepaug River, back when it was still legal to swim there. Ashneon's father, Sean, had been interred separately in the Kelly family plot three counties away. His mother, Katie Kelly Quay, had seen to that. Shamaquin was known to the Kelly clan only as "that tramp who ruined the boy's life." Her son's final resting place lay snugly beside Saint Patrick's Church—well away from the heathen graves of Sean's father's people.

When asked about her granddaughter Ashneon, Katie's standard reply was, "I'm respectin' me boy and consider that a folly best forgotten," followed by the skyward launch of a juicy hawker, eventually splattered upon the unsuspecting ground. Sean never contacted his daughter from beyond. Winay said that was because his folks would not permit it. Any talk about the Irish relatives made Winay shudder from head to toe.

Ashneon leaned against the boulder and closed her eyes. No matter how many times she visited her mother on the other side, she never grew accustomed to the freefall between time and space. But today, the trip was different—more like a short hop down a couple of stairs. Still, the sharp, whistling sounds of the afterlife kicked in right on queue.

There was Shamaquin, amorphous as always, shimmering and writhing in liquid gray shadows as if trapped in a puddle of mercury. Only today she was not smiling.

"Mother, what's wrong?" asked Ashneon. Then, "it's about me and Peter, isn't it?"

"You need to observe things more carefully. Remember the lesson of the mask. I won't be able to contact you for a bit. But don't worry. We'll chat again at length, by and by."

Shamaquin began to fade. Was she crying?

"But mother, wait! I don't understand."

Tomuck sat whittling on the droopy front steps of the Weekum House, its cedar shingles graying and worn in patches, much like himself. Both he and the house were brittle-dry, woodsy beings, determined to hold on to what was real. Each wore natural decay like a medal of honor.

Sometimes, whittling seemed as lazy as lounging in front of the cy, but its purpose was quite the opposite. Whittlers touched, smelled, tasted, understood the true essence of a tree. When Tomuck scooped out wooden bowls and spoons, he became maple, ash, and oak.

He said, "when I whittle, my roots plunge deep into the belly of Mother Earth and she speaks to me, tells me where this world is going and where she's already been."

Tomuck was often quite eloquent—in a rawhide sort of way.

"Whooop, look who's back," Tomuck greeted Ashneon from his whittling post on the front steps.

The old tree man was always the same.

"Yes, I'm back, Uncle," Ashneon shouted. "I had to check in with you-know-who."

Tomuck's knotty fingers fumbled the crooked knife, sending it tumbling into a cloud of dirt at the foot of the front steps.

"Garnukee! Mejeegun!"

Ashneon skittered past the trail of profanities and bumped right into Peter, his cornsilk ponytail brushed against her ear as he whispered, "your uncle hasn't said one word to me since you left. I don't think he believes any good can come of our research."

Tomuck barged in on them, lugging a birchbark bundle

under one arm. "Your people better stop that messing with the natural world, Peter," he ordered. "I see that now they've succeeded in cloning the wooly mammoth, they're looking at trying it out on sea monsters. Be dredging for Ogo Pogo before you know it. Foolishness! You know what's gonna happen if you don't stop?"

"Clearly, nothing good can come of it. I agree, Chief," Peter responded obediently, accustomed to assuming responsibility for any foolish action of the white scientific community. Tomuck never left the mountain and Peter knew he was the only squirming white man that the Yantuck Medicine Chief could regularly interrogate.

"I always meant to ask, was you ever 'service'?" asked Tomuck.

"Excuse me, sir?" coughed Peter.

"Service—you know—military. Air force, Marines, that new space branch. Never can remember what it's called. Any of 'em?"

Tomuck was pouring steaming cawhee into a thick, white navy mug. He always drank it black.

"No sir, never."

Peter gulped at the old man's starched shirt sleeves and gleaming patent leather shoes, an impeccable ensemble that screamed "United States Armed Forces."

Tomuck hissed, "United States been in so many little wars the last few decades, I figured just about everybody must have served, protected this land. Must be a reason you weren't picked. Hmm? 'Course, you're a scholar, not a fighter. Here, boy, let me show you something. C'mere, c'mere."

The Chief winked at Ashneon's clenched teeth and waved Peter toward him.

"Take a look at this and tell me what you see," insisted Tomuck.

Inside the curly bark lay a stiff medicine pouch, its parched leather crackling. Tomuck picked apart the brittle edges to expose his prize: a triangular quartz crystal stone, about the size of a thumbnail.

"That's a beauty," Peter crooned, rolling it between his fingers. "Looks like a textbook levanna projectile point."

"A la-who, which? Aaaach. Forget it. You kids continue with whatever you're doing. Winay'll be down in a minute."

Tomuck shook his head, "La-vin-ia, of all the foolishness." The old man slapped the stone into Ashneon's palm.

"Something you should have, Medicine Girl. An old medicine friend gave it to me, and you're gonna need it."

"What Tribe is it from?" she asked.

"That don't matter, girl!" His boot whacked the floor three times. "Medicine People are the same everywhere! Different spots just got different doors to the same big, wide universe. Real medicine don't know points on a compass. It don't even come from Mother Earth alone. You women get so caught up with your Mother Earth you forget all about your fathers and grandfathers in the sky. Medicine is about touching the whole cosmos. Can't balance infinity from a single mountaintop on one lonely planet and expect the great universe to fall in line. The Mountain is important but you gotta free yourself up, learn how to fly, touch the stars. Haven't I told you this before? Now you just observe, concentrate, and remember a little better and you'll be all right," he directed and stomped away.

In the light of the kitchen window, it became obvious that this was no levanna point. The three-sided stone was clear as glass, except for a milky oval eye, just off center, that played with the light when you peered through it.

Ashneon clapped a hand over her mouth. This was no arrowhead. This was an eyestone, a legendary amulet capable of seeing many things.

How did she know that? And where did it come from? This

rock was different from any found in New England, yet it clearly came from a place beside the sea.

A strange limerick flashed thru her mind:

There once was a stone with an eye
Through which all chosen spirits could spy
Without effort or task
It could rip any mask
Be it ruse, trick, deception, or lie.

What was that all about?

Ashneon followed the trail of grumbling profanities back toward Tomuck. One Yantuck phrase clearly referenced Peter's lack of something. But she couldn't quite translate it.

"Hey, I'll take good care of the, um, 'levanna point,'" she assured her great-uncle.

They both chuckled and gagged on the absurdity of it all. This was her last chance to raise his spirits.

"Museum opens at ten today. You all set?" Ashneon perked up. Tomuck darkened.

"Ain't going up," he grumped.

"But Winay can't manage by herself anymore."

"You go up, then," snapped Tomuck. "Might learn somethin'. Bookery ain't nothin'. Can't eat a book, can ya? Can't build a shelter out of it. Can't transcend this dimension with it. Can't see the future in it. Can't . . ."

"Oh my, oh, my . . ." Winay cut in, swinging a basket full of overripe, wild strawberries. As the sweet fragrance wafted in, the tensions in the room began to settle.

"What do you mean you're not going up?" she went on. "These young people have valuable work to do. Besides, you don't want to disappoint all the folks coming here just to see the great Medicine Chief."

She always got him with that one. Tomuck thought he was the only Indian man in the world who people really wanted to see. In fact, most of the time, he thought he was the only Indian man left in the world, period.

"Fine, I heard you. I'll be up in a few minutes."

A lush strawberry slurped past his lips.

"Not bad. Not bad at all."

The juices rolled over his tongue. Somewhat rejuvenated, Tomuck settled onto the front steps to do a little whittling before the day's visitors arrived. As soon as Peter excused himself to use the facilities, Tomuck hailed the two women through the screen door, "Pshhht. Pshhht! Look!"

"What's he want now?" Winay asked.

Ashneon shrugged.

"Come over here, quick. You two women are so busy with nothing, you almost missed it. Come and have a look out the window at something real for a change," he whispered.

A checkerboard of red-winged blackbirds rose above the hedge, joined in a perfect V as one great bird.

"*Quay, Quay,*" Winay bid them well.

Tomuck slumped as the birds fell out of sight.

"Did I miss something?" asked Peter, emerging from the bathroom.

"Well, I'm set. That's all I needed. I'm up," said Tomuck, bolting upright and bouncing out the door declaring, "Lavinia! Oh my darling Lavinia! Of all the fool things."

He surged up the path to the family museum, clapping his hands and singing, "Oh My Darlin' Lavinia" to the tune of "Clementine."

Ashneon was still beaming at the empty lawn when Peter broke in.

"So," Peter asked Winay, "have you had a lot of visitors from the media lately?"

Winay cleared her throat repeatedly, but Ashneon did not budge, so she interjected,

"Seems like it never stops! Must think these old folks hold the secrets of the universe. Ridiculous. I don't know who came up with this Oracle business in the first place."

That woke Ashneon up. Those words were spears. Barely a year ago, an article entitled "The Weekum Medicine Legacy" had appeared in *The Journal of Indigenous Peoples,* coauthored by Ashneon Quay and Dr. Peter Lymmel. The two of them had presented that paper at the American Anthropological Association's annual meeting in Washington, D.C.

"All right, you two." She poked Ashneon's arm. "Just go on doing what you're doing and don't pay any attention to Tomuck. Let me know what you find out, though. Reminds me of my university days. I'll be down around lunchtime. I got to keep an eye on the old man. His mouth's worse than ever."

Winay meandered up the mountain, stopping every few feet or so, first to greet a droopy young boneset shoot, next to coax a struggling patch of joe pie weed, and finally, to console a hopeless weecup sapling. Each was as much Winay's faltering child as Shamaquin had once been.

Meanwhile, Ashneon remained fixed to the window, her long fingernails digging deeply into the peeling sill. Outside, one frantic renegade blackbird swooped around, and headed right for the open kitchen window.

A fractured cry tore open Yantuck Mountain.

"What? Ashneon, what's wrong? You see a ghost?" Peter finally looked up and shrieked, "Oh shit!"

His cy headset banged to the ground as the bird's wing brushed his face.

Ashneon pleaded, "Oh bird, this is no good for you or us! You don't belong here. Peter, help me get him out, NOW!"

"Don't freak! You *like* birds! Remember?" he screeched.

Peter lunged to shoo the intruder out the door with a book. "No. Seriously, no, Peter, you don't understand. He's got to get out of the house now!"

"Ash, take it easy and hand me my jacket. I'll get him."

As Peter dove toward the blackbird, he tripped on a loose sandal strap and smashed his knee on the step. On its way upstairs, the bird finished him off with a nasty peck on the head.

"Ow! I don't think I can get him. I hope you're not going to freak out all day over this. We've got a lot of work to do. This doesn't mean anything," Peter scolded.

"You ignorant bastard. It means everything!" Ashneon rushed past him upstairs.

Time had stopped flowing, frozen, inside icy doom. No one could say how many moments passed in the world beyond after the thump-a-thump of lively blackbird wings ceased, but on Yantuck Mountain time stood still. Seconds, minutes, perhaps an eternity whizzed by before a blood curdling shriek set the clocks ticking again.

There lay a dirge, an age-old omen disguised as a taxidermic wonder, a silent shell with no obvious sign of damage. The oracle's stiff breast ballooned atop the tan fringe of a Navaho rug, its red-tipped wings neatly snapped shut beneath a head that shone like a perfect feathered mask.

FINN

ANCIENT IRISH STORY

Long ago, a giant named Finn McCool made his home atop a lofty mountain beside the sea. He was in love with a beautiful woman giant who lived far across the waterway, so he built a path of stones to unite them. With this gesture, he won her heart and they lived together for many years.

When the age of giants neared its end, the couple decided to move on. They mounted a staircase made of fog and ascended into the clouds. Some say that on foggy days, the giant couple can still be seen traveling to and fro upon the staircase, reminding both leprechaun and daoine, alike, of those who came before them.

CHAPTER 5
PILGRIMS

Some had never seen a tree.

An immature sapling?

Perhaps. Maybe even something as big around as a hefty leg, but not a tree: a thing that towered, shaded, dug roots into deep spaces unknown to human beings. Nothing even close.

The Boulderton middle-schoolers marveled through muddy bus windows at the thick band of maple, oak, ash, pine, and cedar. The entire eastern seaboard had only a few such tree stands left.

The Yantuck Indian Tribe could not be credited with the survival of this tree haven. It remained on their mountain not because the Indians had succeeded in protecting the natural world, but because they had failed at becoming good corporate Americans. Most trees, at the foot of their mountain down in Fire Hollow were swallowed during the casino's final gasp. Trees remained higher up because tribal funds expired before the chainsaws could dice up the mountain.

Every fall, schools were enticed to power up their beat-up buses for trips up the mountain. The allure of the Weekums and the trees rendered the Yantuck Museum the local equivalent of Disneyworld. This particular group had made only a short trek from three exits up the highway.

As soon as the seventh- and eighth-graders drained out of the bus, they crashed into one another, whirring about in delirious worship at the foot of the glorious trees. The spry Medicine Chief shook their hands, steadying the dizzy visitors. A brown-noser with rainbow braidlets keeled over backwards onto the granite steps, attempting to show her teacher a sky-high oak with a waist as big around as a bus tire.

51

The journey up Yantuck mountain was never easy and there were always those who required special attention. This time, two girls with matching haircuts and portable breathing tanks scaled the mountain in a beat-up golf cart. It did not matter how you climbed the mountain. Whether walking, riding, or flying, all visitors experienced an extraordinary rite of passage when they entered the portal that separated the Yantuck Museum from the rest of the world.

Tomuck deemed the land beyond the mountain a wasteland, a vast nothingness puddled with continents of exotic outlanders stamped white, yellow, red, or black. It did not matter who they were. To Tomuck Weekum, most people living off the mountain were nothing more than incidentals.

Nonetheless, the old man usually remained gracious to the pilgrims who journeyed to his Mecca. All who visited Yantuck Mountain got what they came for, whether they wanted it or not.

"Aquay," he greeted them. "Welcome to Yantuck Mountain. The Natives who have always lived here live here still; others like you visit, only briefly, as our guests. You won't find much tech here. This is one of those few places not yet conquered by the all-powerful Cy."

Something about that speech was beginning to have a worn-out feeling. Tomuck chose to begin tours beside the region's last stand of mature trees. Both the height of the trees and the steep grade prompted visitors to look and think higher. Those who rushed back down that notorious slope often experienced the most painful lesson of all.

"Now, my niece, Ashneon Quay, the successor to our Medicine Woman Winay Weekum, will lead you up the mountain—s l o w l y. For those of you cityfolk not used to the woods, you will be getting a Yantuck Indian education today. As you can see, this mountain is home to real woodlands, just about the last around. Our people have lived here forever. Many of the trees here are marked, so you can remember their names. Get to know them. Learn what they are used for. Once you do, you will wish to protect them. Each tree has special talents and gifts, just like each of you. White oak makes strong baskets, maple makes tasty spoons, hickory makes supple bows. Pay attention to the unique qualities of each one."

Tomuck scanned the crowd to select his victim. A sunburned boy flicked a pointy tongue and smacked his raw lips.

"You there, beach lover, what's your name?" the old man demanded.

The boy sprayed something down his throat. "John Mason," he sputtered, eyes darting about like a hungry rat. Mason. That name Tomuck had not heard in years. The Mason's were Bolderton's leading family, or had been anyway. Chuck, the family partiarch, was the CEO of Necare Pharmaceutical Corporation—that is, before its trillion dollar settlement over the women's fertility drug Repara. Its success in regenerating rotten middle-aged eggs cost thousands of babies the use of their respiratory systems. Chuck and his wife, Charity, had sired two sons, John and Winthrop, born a thrifty decade apart. John was probably too young to know that his big brother had been the prime suspect in the Big Rock Casino Fire. The police had scraped Winthrop Underhill Mason's DNA off the infamous note sent to casino CEO Ryan Tianu. Funny how Winthrop had enlisted in the Navy shortly thereafter.

"So, Mr. Mason," heaved Tomuck, "what does that sign say?"

"It says—shit, I dunno man. I don't even know what I'm doing here. All this nature is nice. But nobody needs it no more, Chief!"

The boy's bloodshot eyes leapt from peer to peer, soliciting approval. But no one breathed.

"You believe you know a lot of things, son. So it shouldn't be too hard for you to read this sign. You can read, can't you?"

"Nope, can't," snorted the boy. "Just goofin' Chief. I got it. Says 'observe, concentrate and remember.'"

"Now, do observe and watch your step, young man. Nature can be your friend or your enemy depending on your attitude."

Tomuck signaled the pilgrims to further scale the mountain and each gasped as they crested the first rise. A voluptuous vegetable garden boasted mile high flint corn towering over bulging clusters of pink speckled shell beans and obese, lumpy summer squash. Close by, plump, overripe tomatoes split wide open next to tight bundles of green beans and shiny peppers, their climbing sticks teeter-tottering.

Even that bounty was not much compared to pre-casino days when a kaleidoscope of community gardens kept the Yantuck Mountain folk alive. Still, this was the largest cultivation of edible life forms these young cyberbrats had ever seen. This was not how the vegetables *they* ate looked or smelled. None of their families planted gardens anymore. A Mother's Day cup filled with wilted sprouts was agriculture to these kids.

Past the vegetable shrine was the damp-sweet smell of late September, the cleanest scent of New England, dating from a time when the woods were new. The Yantuck Indian Museum seemed every bit as ancient as those woods. Lively vines crept through its windows, seeking free admission to the perpetual circus within. Mice performed highwire acts across roughhewn timbers while spiders trapezed between rafters; and if you looked very closely, you could even detect the artifacts stirring.

Ashneon intervened. "I need to collect all electronic devices at this time. They will be returned at the conclusion of the tour. All the tech you'll find up here is one, old-style telephone for emergencies."

The teacher had been warned about this ahead of time. Many balked at not having their cyberlives in tow and some even canceled trips as a result of the rule. But Tomuck and Winay remained firm. At the Yantuck Indian Museum, everyone played by their rules. They were ready and willing to face off against any silicon invader.

This teacher was not a first-timer. She had performed the tech-check before ever leaving school. Some days, it got ugly.

Tomuck began, "Boys, girls, teachers, please find a seat."

A roar of conversation surrounded the tottery oak benches. Aluminum bleachers and folding chairs were the most primitive seating these kids usually encountered.

"Now, my friend here thinks nature is an old-fashioned thing, that we don't need it anymore. Is that right?"

The sunburned boy thought Tomuck had forgotten about him. He obviously had not heard about Tomuck.

"Well son, what if I tell you that all things are connected and that you are part of nature, like it or not?"

"You mean, cuz I'm king of the food chain?" The boy wheezed and snorted over his wit, rousing a few benighted followers.

"No, I mean we are all stuck in Grandmother Spider's universal web and you never know who she's gonna strike next. Might hit us with a hurricane, or a meteor, or something as simple as this." He thrust out his arm. "Here, take it boy."

The birds fell silent as Tomuck's victim grasped the wampum bear club. The boy's scalp instantly flashed from pink to scarlet, as if ready to burst into flames.

"Hey, w'sup? I feel real sick, man. I gotta sit down." He spritzed more medication down his throat.

In the front row, the recently toppled brown-noser rippled with laughter, jiggling dozens of rainbow braidlets like Times Square ticker tape.

Tomuck had pulled out all the stops. There was wampum in that club and wampum attacks spiritual infection. The boy would be at odds with himself for a few days. But, after a week or so, he would return without his medicine. They always did.

"Son, that was just a little bit of nature talking to you. This wampum here is from quahog clam shells, the sacred gift of the sea. Wampum carries the life force of water, blood of the earth, the world's greatest cleanser. The club also holds the strength of the bear."

"Now, you young people notice there ain't too many bears left on Yantuck Mountain anymore. Why is that?" Tomuck asked the group.

"Probably pollution. Or habitat destruction?" gushed the colorful brown-noser.

"How about murder?" The old Chief spoke right into her trembling chin. "Young lady, a long time ago, there was a whole lot of bears here on this mountain. Then Europeans came and enacted a bounty on them. As the bears became nearly extinct, so too, did the Yantuck people. Why is that? You, sunburn boy, you tell me what you know about white men burning and destroying things on this mountain?"

"I don't know nothin'. Please sir, I ain't feeling so good. Don't ask me no more."

"Anybody besides Mr. Mason?" Tomuck asked smugly.

"The Indians died because they were connected to the bears, the mountain, to all of the natural world. Nature and natural people are linked. Like you and the trees," hissed an unseen voice.

The chief scanned the crowd. The speaker had slipped by him.

"Ashneon, you take over for a minute and tell these young people about those trees over there. You have your own special one, I believe."

The chief circled the crowd.

"Certainly, Chief. Boys and girls, near me you see a row of red cedar trees. These trees are sacred to our people. When a Yantuck Indian child is born, we plant a tree for him or her here on the mountain. In this way, we journey through our lives together, growing with the trees, and if all goes well, they continue here long after we are gone. It is our duty to care and provide for the trees, not vice-versa. They are our ancestors. They were here long before us and will remain long after we are gone."

Standing beside her towering cedar made Ashneon queasy, even though it was nothing compared to the height of Tomuck and Winay's trees.

Tomuck cut in, "After the indoor tour with my sister, Medicine Woman Winay Weekum, you will come back outside to visit the Longhouse. Remember to take a good look at its shape."

He domed his hands like the Longhouse roof while bobbing and weaving through the group.

"Everything is rounded in the natural world. Where do you suppose they got the design for them new starships, hmmm?" said Tomuck. His black eyes sparked and their walls came tumbling down.

"Now, you kids haven't lived with too much nature around, but you do watch the nature channels on the cy. Don't you?" he continued. "So tell me, what is the number one law of nature?"

The colorful brown-noser flailed a boney arm in search of redemption. But Tomuck tried one of the Yantuck kids.

"You with the braid, you look like about eighth grade."

The other kids all nodded.

Tomuck continued, "Tell, me young man, what's the number one law of nature?"

Someone was whispering to the boy over his shoulder.

"Survival," he responded.

Even most tribal kids usually got that wrong.

"So to survive, creatures sometimes need to hide," said Tomuck, with both eyebrows raised. He craned his neck nearly full circle to stalk the shadowy whisperer.

"Know something about survival, young lady?" Tomuck had tagged the informer from behind. "Stand up and tell the class your name."

She could not deny her Chief.

"I am Anaquah Tianu. And, uh, I am standing sir."

Close by stood an equally miniscule boy, head boiling over with fiery red curls and feet shoed in green fabric that curled up at the toes. He jabbed Anaquah's rib and muttered, "You tell 'em Colleen!"

Tomuck stifled a gasp as he bent way down to speak to the young woman, "So your first name means 'star,' and your last name means 'fine.'"

One of the townie boys snorted, "Yeah, check out that fine tattoo!"

Tomuck glanced at the shiny, golden star on the girl's shoulder. "Anaquah, how old are you?"

Anaquah fidgeted with her drooping glasses. "Twelve, Chief," she replied.

"So, in those twelve years, what have you heard about your people's survival?

"That over time, we have had to change our ways to survive, including having to learn to use the cy."

Tomuck smiled tightly. "And what exactly do you think that you can learn from the cy?"

Anaquah dove in and did not come up for air, "We can learn how to destroy the natural world or, I believe, how to save it. The choice is ours. The cy is made up of tiny things with big implications, much the same as DNA and viruses. Smallpox was one of those tiny things and look what it did to us back in the 1600s. Look what it could still do. A cy-chip is a lot smaller than these trees, but it can hold more information than paper made from a million of them. The components of the cy are small but powerful and we had better make friends with them, make them work for good, or they will destroy the natural world and us along with it. We have to change, Chief. We have to get past our cyphobia. We Yantuck Indians should be accustomed to change and realize that technology and nature are not natural enemies."

Benches creaked. Whispers swished though the crowd. The fiery-haired boy had folded his arms and begun nodding furiously, like a proud papa. Now they were listening.

"I see," said Tomuck. "But I am sure you understand that not all change for our people has been good—like the way our people changed so much they forgot about the natural world altogether for a while. What have you learned about that part of your tribal history?" he asked.

"Well, my father, Ryan, told me about how our people nearly destroyed this reservation, and that all we were able to save was the mountain. He says you saved the people and the mountain, Chief."

Tomuck rubbed the back of his neck.

"Thank you, Ms. Tianu. I will consider your words." He whispered low, " Send your father my regards."

"All right, everyone, time to go inside the museum," said Ashneon. "Follow me please. LET'S LINE UP AT THE FRONT ENTRANCE OF THE MUSEUM TO TAKE OUR TOUR WITH MEDICINE WOMAN, WINAY WEEKUM."

The group stumbled two by two into the odd brew of mothballs, damp stone, and rotting wood that was the Yantuck Museum. Even the most die-hard cyberbrats would experience a moment when they wanted to inhale that musty aroma forever. The stone, wood, and beaded artifacts were gathered in tight, anxious bundles, like the runners at Skeezucks's track meets, each desperate to burst forth from the pack and showcase their individual worth.

"Aquay, greetings," said Winay. "Welcome. This is the room we Yantucks call home."

The cedar talking stick whirled above her head like a magic wand. Tomuck had carved it from a living branch of the last chestnut tree on the mountain. Its charred tip once poked around cinders in the Weekums' old woodstove. Tomuck said that tree had chosen to become a teacher, so he had granted its wish.

Winay removed a mask with infinite black eyes from the peg board and cradled it with her frail, kindling fingers as she told its story. Meanwhile, Ashneon was silently bemoaning the museum's profusion of organic matter as a preservation nightmare. Her internship at the Nadwick Curation Center had taught her more than she ever wanted to know about the fragility of aging wood. How not to handle it too much, how to freeze away bugs, how to thwart the natural erosive cycle of things. But Winay would hear none of it. No one was going to freeze her friends and upset the balance.

The Medicine Woman excavated deeply within an old whaling trunk and pulled out an enormous hickory bow, far too long to have conceivably fit inside. The bow trick was obviously just a clever attention-grabber, since she laid it down without explanation and moved on to the next item.

"Here we are. Let's listen to some of these artifacts and see what they can tell us about themselves." The students snickered and the teachers smiled condescendingly. When Winay finally emerged from rummaging and mumbling, she was dangling three dainty oak baskets along her wistful arm.

"These baskets tell me they have been used to hold offerings for the great Bawba." Each was painted with amber triangles, leaves and stars.

"You may not know Bawba," Winay continued. "But you will one day. He is the leader of the Beachers—those ancient giants who protect the plants and trees."

Winay paused a moment for the inevitable chuckles.

Beside Anaquah, the fiery-haired lad was bobbing up and

down beneath a flailing arm. Winay's eyes popped when she finally noticed his feet.

"Medcin Ladee, Oh Medcin Ladee, Doon't ye haf leetle peeple, as well?" asked the wee, rusty-headed lad.

"Young man you're not with the class and you're not from around here. Are you?" snipped Winay.

The boy did not respond.

"Well, as you know, in the natural world there is always balance," the old woman went on in a noticibly haughtier tone. "So where you have giants there must, indeed, be Little People. But, in my opinion, Little People are a nuisance, what with the way they sneak about and make mischief. You do know what I mean, don't you dear?" quipped Winay.

"Well!" He turned toward Anaquah, huffing and puffing, "Thot I coot hep ye, Colleen. But thay're ull yuz. Be back fer yew sun enuf! No goot Beacher-lovers!"

"Colleen?" Anaquah did not have a clue who this strange boy thought that she was; but she choked as poofs of sparkles trailed behind him on his way out the door.

Anaquah and Ashneon shrugged at one another.

Most of the class missed the odd exchange between the Medicine Woman and the fiery-haired upstart, having already bustled over to take turns peeking inside the enchanted, painted baskets. Those curious enough to shine flashlights inside found there were dark areas near the bottom that remained unseen.

The stylish duo in the golf cart giggled into the baskets, then stopped breathing momentarily when the basket giggled back. Prior to that retort, they had been fully prepared to offer themselves up as Bawba's vestal virgins. Now they wondered about the real price of becoming Bawba's women.

Winay refocused the class's attention. "Now, let's look and see what else is inside this trunk."

She tossed a tattered, beaded change purse into the air before retrieving a ragged cloth doll propped on a painted cedar stand that depicted a bush engulfed in flames of red, gold, amber, and blue. The doll's cheeks looked water-stained.

"Isn't she sad?" asked Winay. "This old woman tells the story of Fire Hollow. See how she turns her back to the fire?" The group crowded tight, sharing one another's hot, curious breath.

Winay resumed in a whisper, tilting her ear toward the itsy bitsy doll woman. "She tells me that many places carry the spirit of fire, like Fire Hollow right here at the foot of this mountain. See how the doll turns away from the flame? That is because the flame engulfs a plant and does not burn, making it a dangerous flame: one that we call Star Fire. Fear it. Respect its power. As with the fiery stars above, blue flames are young and burn short and hot but red fire is lasting. Such stellar flames are capable of bringing forth life or death."

Flames flickered in the visitor's eyes. They would be more careful from now on, aware of new perils.

The Medicine Woman beckoned them to follow her into the Stone Room. At that moment, most of them would have followed her anywhere. Only Anaquah hesitated, quivering slightly. Peering out from a top shelf in the corner of the room, she spied the black eyes of a tall, skinny, wooden man, dressed in a green suit and top hat—whose eyes were following her.

In the Stone Room, there were no crackling woven baskets with blood-red splints, no threadbare velvet purses dripping with bright pony beads—just grizzly, gray rocks that would last forever. It was Ashneon's least favorite part of the museum.

"These stones are what remain of the ancient past," Winay continued. "They truly know how to survive. Look closely at the arrowheads, spears, and axes. Some are a few hundred years old, others tens of thousands."

This room took only a few moments to view, but the carved stones shoved the students back eons in time.

"Touch that spear," encouraged Winay. "It's ten thousand years old. Looks like brand new, doesn't it? Perhaps that's not really as long ago as you think. These stones know that time is a brobdingnagian sea to be swum only by those who do not crave the safety of any shore." The teachers all made a note to look up that word.

The old woman concluded, "A journey through time is at once the most challenging and worthiest of adventures."

Not until later would the group fully process Winay's wisdom. Tomuck summoned them to the Longhouse for the conclusion of their tour. There, a bleached horse skull hung from a rotting post as a careful reminder. He bid them farewell as they regrouped according to bus number, desperately collecting their fractured thoughts before returning to the Land Beyond.

The teachers were spent. They rarely hung in this long. All but one had already fled downhill, desperate for a cyberfix.

"Hang on to the railing and walk slowly as you go down the mountain. Be careful not to stumble, boys and girls," cautioned Ashneon.

The young people's steps were not as sure as when they first arrived: a damaged matrix affords few footholds. But Tomuck had provided them with other safeguards—the knowledge of how to observe, concentrate, and remember. As they passed the droopy fruit trees and the lush vegetable garden, new mental pathways burst open. Many wanted to skip, but resisted the urge, aware that their new knowledge inclined them to stumble.

Their guide warned one last time, "go slowly down the steep path. Getting there takes the time that it takes."

After they had gone, Ashneon shook the birch bark collection basket.

"Fifty dollars," she whispered almost imperceptibly.

A wooden Indian head nickel with Tomuck's mark on it rattled beneath the teacher's check.

"Oh Tomuck!" she gasped.

The collection basket was the place for the white man's tribute offering—a dollar in spring, summer, winter or fall. Most everyone left something. Tribespeople brought Tomuck the greatest gifts of every season: blue shell crabs in July, bushels of corn in August, venison in October, strawberries in June. After all, no one wished to be denied the favor of Tomuck and Winay Weekum, especially now that they were about to become Oracles.

CHAPTER 6
LESSONS OF FALL

"The German Duchess is up visiting your great-uncle again," sneered Winay.

"Not anymore. She's slithering back down the path right now," countered Ashneon. "Couldn't even captivate him for a full morning this time."

The visitor looked like an aging Bavarian beer commercial. Although still quite pert for sixty-something, her ashen hair was strewn about in one last, frantic quest for lost blondeness. Some of the loveliest creatures still solicited Tomuck—though he was, now, merely a withered old man. Why they bothered was the question. He hardly paid them any mind. After all, they were merely incidentals.

This latest incidental had fallen clear out of sight, receded back to her alien origins. Without her, the view was sublime. The path up the mountain was lined with splintered railroad ties. A sickly apple tree languished over the sweat-polished railing; not a single fruit dangled from her autumn branches. The neighboring pear tree was also hopelessly sterile. Winay claimed they could not reproduce because of their foreign origin.

Tomuck's German lady friend had appeared at the same time last year. This was an energetic season for all creatures, a last hurrah before the mountain lapsed into its seasonal nap.

"I'm heading up to attack the fingerprints on those cases. I'll also try to clean out some of the mouse chewings I saw inside the stone room."

Ashneon scooped her cleaning supplies into a bucket. Winay had never once had to ask her granddaughter to tidy up. The young woman whisked through dirt and clutter just like she stormed through everything else.

"You're asking for a lecture today," Winay warned as the screen door banged shut.

Inside the museum, Tomuck was tossing his head about whistling "This Land is your Land."

"Uncle, the cleaning crew is here!"

On this day, listening to Tomuck lecture did not seem like a half-bad thing to do.

"I heard a rumor down at the tribal office that you have a secret crush on that Lakota cyporter, Sunny Buffalo. They say she wants to meet you too," nudged Ashneon.

"Don't doubt it." Tomuck pulled up his skeleton, almost straight, and smoothed a hand across what had once been his chest. "I'm ready for her," he winked and screwed up his nose at the untidy braids clipped on top of her head.

When she was devoid of glamor, it always meant she was up to something. Ashneon frequently sported exotic, but nonetheless meticulous, hairstyles: three braids down her back, looped braids falling from the crown of her head, a ring of braids circling her brow, twisted rows of braids graduating from small to large. But not today.

"Tomuck, don't you think her show, 'The Way of the White Buffalo,' is trash? Why would any self-respecting Indian feed that New Light Oracle garbage?"

Ashneon nestled into a torn seat cushion, forcing out the stuffing from one end. Tomuck had chosen a spot by the window where the cushion was still intact, though faded to a raw, fleshy pink. The distant highway swished lightly by as he munched his bologna sandwich and chips. He sprinkled a mini salt shaker onto his beer and handed the frothy glass to his grand-neice.

"Here, have some. You need it. It'll cool you down."

She took a hefty slug.

"You eat yet?" he asked.

"I had some leftover corned beef and cabbage hash."

"Well, at least you eat real food and not that New Light garbage most gals your age pick at." He laughed a little too heartily. "Now, I got to say it, Ashneon. It's time you started spending less time in them books and more time with what's real. This museum, this is reality. Right here. My isle of golden dreams."

"Tell me something, Tomuck. Is it my imagination or is this museum not really a museum at all? Sometimes, it seems just like an extension of the woods."

He slapped his knee. "Now, you're getting it! That's it! Listen here, Medicine Girl. Every lesson you need is right here. You don't need them books, especially the ones on medicine, 'less you want to learn useless parlor tricks. All you need is right here. I don't care if you call yourself an Oracle, a witch, or what-have-you. Don't matter none what real medicine is called, or where it comes from. What matters is that it be real. Anyhow, you'll be in touch with the real thing before you know it." His voice trailed off. Then, "So long as you quit keeping company with Lyman and his kind."

"You know his name is Lymmel and I only study books with him to learn more about these things," she defended.

"Well, no use wasting my breath. You'll see for yourself before too long," Tomuck huffed.

Down slid the last bite of sandwich.

"It's easy for you to criticize my bookery when Winay is nowhere to protect me," snapped Ashneon. "At least I don't spend every minute on the cy like most people my age."

"Got that right. But listen here. It was people desperate to get at what's in them books that got this cy business going in the first place. I'm still gonna say it. You've got all the research you need right up here." His index finger attempted to drill straight down for emphasis, but the last, arthritic digit veered westward off toward the horizon.

Tomuck lifted the bear club off the shelf and declared, "Touch this with those same mental muscles you use to visit your dead folk and you'll find out what I'm talking about. Try it. You're ready now. Focus on what's inside."

A flashback from a previous encounter with the club doubled her over. The last time Tomuck had her touch it was three A.M., the night of the junior prom. "For your own good," he had growled. The next day, she awoke in a slimy gold and amber sea of Jameson and tortillas.

This time, things would be clearer.

As soon as her fingertips met the wood, the room slowly unfolded into a maze of hidden pictures. Inside Bawba's offering basket, she viewed a swirling soup of tear-stained women. High above, a thin, wooden doll, all dressed in green, tossed his mangy head back and forth, while humming a familiar jingle. The club in her hand snarled at him and she released it briefly, before boldly picking it up again. Each museum artifact appeared animated and possessed of a being or beings that served as its keeper, or group of keepers, all locked within the object yet still able to view their surroundings, as though each was drifting about inside a transparent soap bubble.

Yes! That was it! The artifacts were like children's bubbles blown about on a clear spring day, free-floating glassy balls all streaked with pink cheeks and blue skies, carrying the stories and reflections of all those they passed by, each bubble beginning its existence with hope, beauty, and innocence; until, after a while, they all popped.

"Here," she returned the club to Tomuck and collapsed onto a cedar bench, blinking away splattered bubbles.

"Put them all away now," he instructed.

The last bubble dissolved into the ether.

"What was that?" she asked, her back resting on the museum's granite face.

"That was what I have been trying to tell you about. Didya think your grandmother was joking about having spoken to these artifacts? Today you took your first step down that path. I'm glad of it, too. I couldn't wait no longer. I don't have forever to make sure that you understand some things. Those faces you saw," he pointed to the artifacts. "They all want to meet you. Every one of them can tell you a story. The club is just one way to open the door. There are plenty of other ways. But I think you've had enough of the heavy stuff for today. You're on your way, now. You won't need no more convincing. No more help, neither!"

This was one of those rare moments when Ashneon sat still. She knew there was more to come.

"And another thing," he resumed smugly. "I know your grandmother Winay's a great one for telling you stories about other people's magic. But remember: some folks pass on the tales, others do the deeds. You ain't just some humdrum story-teller. You're a storymaker, more so than either of us two old-timers. You're one of them that makes the magic they tell about for generations to come. You've already made a good start at becoming a legend, what with your odd eyes and regular visits to the dead and all."

He rubbed his chest and twisted up his face. "But frankly, vis-iting the dead ain't that useful to the living. You need to connect with the magic hidden in the things still of this world if you want to help it. Which brings me to my point, Ashneon: you can be a lot more than just a bookish passer on of useless information. Don't read them books no more. That's the simple stuff. Reading objects—now *there's* the challenge and the reward."

Tomuck sucked in with the kind of breath that meant the grand finale was at hand. The pause was intended to allow his words sufficient time to penetrate the shields of her college education.

"It's a different kind of study, a different science," he resumed. "Books describe the mere surface of these treasures."

He cast an open hand toward the object-beings.

"Could—" Ashneon started, but Tomuck interrupted. "Don't ask me to show you how to read 'em, cuz I can't hardly do it no more myself. Garnering that sort of energy could take me out of this world and straight on over to the other side, and unlike you, mine would be a one-way trip."

Tomuck struck a rigid, cigar-store pose.

"Does all this have something to do with the way the woods and the museum sometime seem like one and the same thing?" Ashneon asked.

"Now she's got it!" He pounded his fist onto the exhibit case. "I've told you what I know about these woods, because knowing them means knowing this museum, knowing yourself, and knowing all creation. Everything you could ever want is right here. You know how I tell folks that all you need is a knife and an ax and you can live on this mountain forever. With those tools you can work with the trees, make your wigwam, bows and arrows, get plenty of good things to eat—even though you don't hunt. Winay did well teaching you about the woodland plants and nuts and whatnot. That information will see you through Armageddon. 'Course, you might be a scrounging, vegetarian weakling like Peter, but you'd make it. Besides, she taught you about all those folks who can help you from the spirit world—Beachers and the like. Though I understand you and ol' Bawba have some issues," He jabbed her forearm and shifted his weight, "'Course, there is a serious problem, though. I truly wonder, Ashneon . . ."

The blue flames of her eyes flared up.

He continued, "I don't know how well you know the trees,

and they are what make the woods. You can remove anything else and still have woods, unless you remove the trees. Maybe it's time you started paying less attention to saving what's written on paper and more attention to saving the source of that paper. Here endeth the lesson."

Ashneon was silent for a long moment. Then, "Tomuck, I think somehow I always knew that the museum and the woods were the same and that these woods hold all that we are as Yantuck people. I also knew that when they go, we go, too. But what I didn't know was that these woods and these artifacts are a window into other worlds and beings."

"There now, I hope you don't feel you've missed an afternoon of reading. Just keep working on that new skill you tried out today. It will get more powerful right away, so don't get too fired up or you'll get burned. Books'll just slow you down. But you do what you want. You will anyway."

Dust billowed from each thunderous footfall as Ashneon bulldozed back down the mountain toward the Weekum House. She was about to finish college and her real education had only just begun. The amber crescent moon dangled above her head, like a razor-edged sickle in the twilight sky.

CHAPTER 7

BELLS

The pint-size ball jar brimmed with a glorious mixture of pineo mushrooms, stewed tomatoes, cubanelles, long hots, basil, and sliced garlic. This batch was a little too fiery for everyone but Tashteh. The milder jars were set aside for Aquinnee and Skeezucks as a special Sunday treat.

Ashneon presented Tashteh with the scrumptious prize.

"Oh yeah, Ash! You did this batch up right. A little deer meat and some baked beans with these babies and I'm good to go!" He boomed a great belly laugh, "Still can't believe how many we found this year. Tell you what, let's go for a drive and we'll stop at a burial ground I want you to see. But only one. You wearing okay shoes?"

Tomuck watched the young couple scurry toward the pickup and an unpleasant surge raced through his worn-out old heart. Becoming Medicine Chief had nixed so many other possibilities. The best way to chase away those dusty, might-have-beens was to cozy up to a nice, cold Budweiser.

"Oh, Tashteh, I almost forgot to tell you. What a day I had yesterday with Tomuck!"

"What did the old man do now? Besides tell you to send me back to my own side of the river?" he sniffed and turned away.

"Actually," Ashneon tugged at his sleeve. "He quite likes you compared to most other men."

"By that remark, I presume you are offering Peter Lymmel the undeserved courtesy of being called a man?"

Ashneon chomped down on her lip and prayed it was not bleeding.

"Anyway," she recovered, "something's different about

Tomuck lately. He sleeps up at the museum, almost all the time, and yesterday he talked to me straight, no riddles, parables, nothing. He taught me how to talk to the artifacts, or almost taught me. Something happened, anyway."

"That sounds like your people. What exactly did he say? Oh, hold on. I want to pull over, right up ahead here, before we pass the spot. There it is. That old burial ground around the corner. Something about it has been calling me."

"Wait. Listen, Tashteh. He handed me the bear club and said 'use those same mental muscles you use when you talk to your dead folk', or something like that."

"The wampum-studded bear club?" Tashteh lowered his voice.

Ashneon nodded, "So I touched it, and suddenly the room got real crowded."

"Oh. We're here. It's just down Awdee Street," reported Tashteh.

"Wow. This place is odd. We'll talk about my experience later," Ashneon concluded.

Tashteh offered his hand to help her exit the truck, but Ashneon hesitated. What he really offered was a lure, capable of reeling in even the most free-spirited catch. There was a magnetic strength there, one that you couldn't get from virtual workouts on the cy, only from native genetics and old-time Indian-living.

When she finally accepted that hand, she appeared blasé, like she was loading a cy program. But her quivering fingers split Tashteh's mouth into a big, white, toothy grin.

Before them lay a smooth sea of gray pavement, broken by a tiny, green island. Beyond it stood a crayola crayon world, rows upon government rows of solar huts in every imaginable color, all put up within the last twelve years. The designer tones of these prefab USS (United States Sun) communities were supposed to make up for what they lacked in character, architectural style, organic building matter, and earthen yards.

Around these housing projects, it was impossible to distinguish where, or if, the pavement ended. The medicine duo parked at the edge of a grassy mound that looked like a miniature volcano erupting through the asphalt. Atop it, three tottering field stones lined up like dominos. When the wind picked up, a gang of crisp leaves circled them in a round dance.

"What an odd knoll," she said. "You're right. There seems to be someone here who is calling me. But these aren't Yantuck burials. Too big. Too old. Look more like Beacher mounds to me. And what about that old shagbark hickory in the middle. It's huge! Those roots will be ripping up the pavement soon. Then bye, bye tree. Can't let anything survive that could mess up the lovely pavement now, can we?"

"Four hundred years old, at least! They can't cut this baby down. It falls under the Arbor Law," asserted Tashteh.

"Sure, like that law's never been broken!"

He stroked its curling leaves. The tree could not hold on much longer.

"It's amazing with all this development that this tree and burial ground made it. One more site to worry about protecting," Ashneon stated flatly.

"Since you never noticed it before and it was always right here, then . . ." Tashteh paused.

"Then you guess I wasn't supposed to see it until now," Ashneon agreed. "Not 'til summer ended, anyway.

"I know it's only November, but we've seen frost already, so ol' Bawba shouldn't be anywhere around," Tashteh concluded. "Someone on the other side must have something to say to you today."

His hazelnut eyes beamed down at her. The pressure was on.

"Just give me a minute to prepare." She inhaled deeply.

The rough bark scratched her hand, but she pushed her palm even further into the tree until all expression deserted her face. The journey had begun. Tashteh filled his pipe with his special mix, then leaned back against the truck to contact the spirits in his own way. Tashteh Sook and Ashneon Quay each traveled separately, but their purpose was the same.

This time, Ashneon suffered a brain-whipping roller coaster ride, flip-flopping all the way over to the other side before experiencing that great quiet of the afterlife, lacking even the usual soft whistling.

But where was Shamaquin?

The rest of the welcoming committee was also missing. Before her lay only the uncolor of haze, like the drowsy eye of a storm, and in place of the customary otherworldly whistlings, she heard only a faint glasslike tinkling.

Were those bells?

Yes, bells rising to a beautiful ringing. Bells upon beautiful bells. Now suddenly deafening. Jingling and jangling every-where. Sheep's bells, tinkle cones, jingle dresses, hawk's bells, sleigh bells. A tremendous ceremony was underway and the dancers were joining a great circle.

The ringing rose to an unbearable clanging, then fell silent, signaling her forced return. The predictable Big Step back came next, a gigantic trip over time and space followed by the violent sensory blast that always signaled one's return to the living world.

"Are you back?" he asked.

"Yes." Her teeth were chattering. "Tashteh could you hear that? No, I don't suppose you could, but it was incredibly loud."

"Nope, heard nothing. What did you hear?"

"Bells, really loud bells," she replied.

His face fell, "What kind of bells?"

"Dancing bells—you know. Like all the dead were linked in an enormous round dance, calling someone venerable to join them."

CHAPTER 8
THE GREAT MASK

There was so much to learn from the artifacts, so much at stake with New Light Corporation targeting indigenous Oracles. Dusk had barely fallen, but it was time for bed. Yantuck Mountain had become a battle zone again. Every eleven or twelve years or so, it happened in exactly the same way. Tomuck knew the pattern. He once told Ashneon, "Indian life is more like a ball than a circle. It keeps rolling on and on, stopping only briefly, for thrilling bouts of agonizing play."

Ashneon looked in on her grandmother. "Winay, I just wanted to say goodnight. Sorry I haven't had a chance to talk to you all day. Anything new from Nuda, Obed, or the illustrious New Lighters?"

"Nothing new, birdie."

"We don't have much time," she said softly.

"Well, we must accept what we cannot change. Things always turn out for the best. Everything happens for a reason."

Following the overdone cross-stitch litany, Winay lay back and commenced a pattern of disturbing snorting. Meanwhile, Tomuck remained as still as the fresh-cut maple log atop his night stand.

The Weekum House was always restless on Saturdays. But tonight, the air was even pricklier than usual. The thought of an early morning run to see Peter before he left for the American Anthropological Association's conference did not help any. Peter was an unavoidable magnet. Still, the mood was all wrong. That was a good thing, too, since it was critically important to stay out of the mood around Peter.

Responsibility. Obligation. Tradition. Tashteh had been

drilling her lately, insisting that it was time for them both to focus on the task at hand. He would not shirk his duty.

On the night stand, anything that mattered to Ashneon was tucked inside the sea grass sewing basket woven by her mother. Among its hidden treasures was a smokey quartz choker, a twenty-first birthday gift from Tashteh. That necklace seemed just right for the day. It would serve as a careful reminder.

A lemon chiffon blouse, a few bright beads, a little eye glimmer and a dab of perfume for a finishing touch—but only a little. After all, it was best to ask for only a little trouble when visiting Peter.

Clumps of slick leaves, a maze of fractured limbs, and two enormous felled trees coated the road—the remnants of a wild storm. That explained the restless sleep. The car was sputtering and gagging in a bronchial sort of way. Late again on the service appointment, no doubt. An unfamiliar furry-pink carcass lay pasted to the middle of the road. Probably the last of its kind.

The cy beeped and Ashneon skidded a little on the leaves as she answered it.

Winay's voice cracked only slightly on the word "ambulance." Twenty minutes earlier, the lips of those two women had brushed one another's cheeks in a brief goodbye. Now, those same lips held absolutely still, as though silence alone could prevent their world from galloping away.

"What? What happened to him?" Ashneon finally responded.

"Just old age, I'm sure. You know he's been out of sorts lately. Don't you worry. It'll be all right. Just wanted to let you know right away."

"You want me to come get you?"

"Oh, no point to that. I'll hold the fort. You go on and do what you have to do."

"OK. I'll swing by the hospital right away and see how he's doing."

"All right, birdie. That's fine. You know best. Take care."

There was a call waiting.

"Ashneon, it's only me," said Tashteh. " I'm really sorry about Tomuck. The press already heard. It's on the cy. I am truly sorry. I'll be there as quickly as I can."

"Tashteh, relax. The cy will hype anything. Winay didn't seem that worried, she muttered something about old age. He'll probably be all right. This may be a false alarm."

"What, Ashneon?"

"I said, Tomuck is probably fine."

"Where are you?" demanded Tashteh.

"Huh? Right now exactly?"

"Yes, now exactly!"

"I'm just about at the entrance to Thames Memorial."

The townspeople of Boulderton took great pride in the imposing granite edifice of their state-of-the-art hospital. Ashneon always referred to it as "the mausoleum."

"Are you pulled over?" he asked.

"Yes, I'm there already. But I've got to run, to see Tomuck."

"Ashneon, wait a minute. Listen carefully: Tomuck passed on already."

"What? No! But how? Are you sure?"

"I saw it on the cy."

"No, Tashteh, they're wrong. Why didn't Winay? No! Why didn't I see it coming? He was out of sorts. I should have asked him if he was all right!"

Everything was crumbling. Ashneon tore open a package of Kleenex and wiped her last hope onto a soft rose-scented tissue.

"Damn research," she sobbed. "Sometimes I miss what's

right in front of me. Damn that bird, dying in the house. Damn stupid Peter for not catching it. Damn him. Damn him!"

"I'll be there in just a couple of minutes," he assured.

"OK. I'm going in to see him now. Maybe I can talk to him either way. Meet me at the hospital."

Click.

Ashneon focused on the bold red letters of the Emergency Entrance, then the glass sliding doors, then the bone-crushing fear.

Obed must have issued an all point's bulletin. The waiting room was mobbed with New Light cycameras, their sinister glass eyeballs peering out from every imaginable corner.

The woman behind the counter, fielding all media questions, swished back and forth like a poorly trained hula dancer. Ashneon broke into her ridiculous dance. "Excuse me! I'm here to see Chief Tomuck Weekum."

"Yes. They just brought him in. Oh! You're the niece! I'm so sorry. Please have a seat. A counselor will be right with you."

"A counselor!" Ashneon blurted. "Forget it."

"Excuse me," crooned a liquid voice from behind.

Ashneon twirled around to behold a woman with cheeks shining like the sun-drenched Sahara. Her head was wrapped in a fiery turban and her towering mahogany torso was enveloped in metallic gold and amber gauze.

"You must be Ashneon Quay. I am Sigi Malinke. We will speak in another room. This is a difficult time."

Ashneon dove in, "Ms. Malinke, I really don't want to speak to anyone, except my uncle Tomuck. You understand, don't you? And would you please get these cyporters out of here?"

"Yes, immediately." Sigi shooed the media away like swatted flies. "You shall see him just now. But you will not speak to him. No, that will not be possible; for he wears the Great Mask of the Dead. I am sorry. But it is done. Come Ashneon."

"I remember you from somewhere. Where are you from?" Ashneon asked, as they headed toward Tomuck's room.

"It's been some time since I have been from anywhere. But perhaps we have met along the way. I originally hail from Hombori Tondo."

"The mountain in Mali?"

"Ah! You know it." The woman squeezed her hand with the loving firmness of a mother elephant, a great animal large enough to carry any grief. Ashneon shivered at the thought of just how warm that hand felt, and how familiar. Their meeting was no accident.

Gold sparks flickered in Sigi's eyes. "Come now and you will see your uncle," she instructed.

The crowd was swelling like a new injury as Sigi scooped Ashneon into room three. Outside, it was fast approaching prime time for the cyberazzi.

"Ladies and gentleman, here you see Chief Tomuck Weekum's Oracle protégée Ashneon Quay, the woman who talks to the dead, now on her way to visit her lifelong surrogate father—a man who has just this hour journeyed to the other side. And, ladies and gentlemen, this young woman not only talks to the dead, she walks with the dead. That's right. Sources say she regularly visits the afterlife in person."

Ashneon turned to thank Sigi, but she had vanished. In her place stood a sterile, hospital professional.

"Ms. Quay, I am Dr. Noren, the hospital's grief counselor.

"But who . . ." Ashneon glanced all around.

"Your great-uncle passed over en route. I am not sure how he survived this long, with the lung deterioration he had. I don't see why he wasn't given gene therapy before this went too far." The specialist babbled on. "Will you be the one to tell your grandmother? Do you need anything?"

A mint leaf was stitched onto her sleeve, signifying holistic training, including classes in herbal medicine and shamanic ritual healing. Dr. Noren had obviously been hand-selected to deal with this Native case, but she burrowed her nose into her notes and could not stop gulping.

An Indian Medicine Man who talked to the trees was dead right in her hospital. An Indian woman who visited the dead was standing right next to her. She was in the presence of people who touched medicine in ways she had only read about in books or watched on the cy. These were the kind of people who became Oracles, and both of them were ignoring her completely.

The old chief's hand was empty, and that emptiness began to consume the room like a black hole. Sigi was right. He wore the Great Mask of the Dead.

"I'm here, Tomuck, just as I promised. "I can meet you on the other side now, if you call me over. I miss you. I don't know what to do without you. I love you so much, Tomuck. Please talk to me. Talk to me, please."

Over and over, she pleaded in wet waves, her sheer, tear-soaked blouse sticking to her chest in increasingly revealing patches. But Tomuck did not respond. It was time to leave. Ashneon would not provide a sideshow for the online world—now in hot pursuit.

"No, I have no comment," she insisted to them all.

The cyporters stammered and stumbled around Ashneon, ultimately scurrying away, like detoured marching ants. Ashneon denied them the nourishment of a single glib sound bite. Her kind led the resistance, fighting instant information with unwieldy, full-fledged thought. She locked the car door and tuned in to the all-knowing cy.

"That's right. Tomuck Weekum, slated by New Light Corporation to go online later this month as the world's newest Oracle, has just passed over into the spirit world. Preliminary sources say he may be replaced by niece Ashneon

Quay, a young Yantuck woman, who has the ability to speak to the dead—even visit with them on their own turf!

"Uncle, some people say Sachem's Spring is magic, like the fountain of youth."

"They're right, Ashneon. Springs are the life blood of Mother Earth. They run through her veins."

"But that would mean Mother Earth bleeds here at Sachem's Spring."

"Yes, but when you become a woman, you will see that all mothers bleed to give life. Mother Earth is no different. New life, any change in the universe that matters, requires sacrifice. Often, one life needs to be ended to bring forth another life or another way of being."

"That's not fair. There was no reason for my mother to die. You and Winay are Medicine People. Why couldn't you stop it?"

"Nothing and nobody can upset the balance of the universe, child. Medicine People least of all. We are the balancers."

A dull thump on the windshield shook her loose, but only muffled shreds of words seeped through the glass.

"Ash . . . on, Ash . . . on! Unl . . . the v . . . icle! . . . here . . . soo . . . as . . . uld."

Tashteh pried open the door. "Let me drive you back home to the mountain."

Ashneon shifted into the passenger's seat, just as a tidal wave of cyporters crested over the hood. Tashteh was her lifeline.

"Go!" she instructed.

The cy beeped as he squealed away.

"Ashneon, it's Winay. You all right, birdie?"

"I'm fine. I'll be home in just a few minutes. Don't let in any press until I get there."

"I won't. It'll be all right. Everything works out for the best. I know it's hard to believe that, now. You'll see, Birdie. Bye."

"Thank God she knows already, Tashteh. Thank you for driving, for everything."

"Well, it's a heavy day," he said.

"Can anything else happen?"

"Actually, Ashneon, it already has. The elders voted last night to make me the new Patuxet Medicine Man. That's why I was already in your neck of the woods when I heard about Tomuck. I wanted you to be the first to know. Always the good balanced with the bad. I guess you were already on your way somewhere else, and I would have missed you."

Ashneon tugged at her choker, barely managing to spit out the words, "Your people chose well."

Tashteh suddenly seemed miles away. Pain and pride rumbled together inside her stomach. In one day, she had lost two of the most important men in her life to a greater purpose. Of course she still had Peter, the one man in her life whom she could never lose to a higher calling.

"You know what this all means, Ashneon. We are in this battle together now—in more ways than one. I'll help you protect your great uncle's legacy from those Oracle phonies! Just don't even think for a moment that I'll ever leave you."

"Oh no! What about the eulogy?" Ashneon startled.

"That's another bit of harsh news I have for you. About two seconds before I got here, the cyporter said, 'an Oracle-in-training from the Yantuck Tribe would be delivering the eulogy.'"

"Oh, Tashteh, I'll be all right. I always knew I would have to do it some day. Really, I expected this. Don't you think I've heard all their talk about me being the next Oracle, Medicine Woman, or whatever? Today was a shock and it will be hard to get through the ceremony, but I know I can do it. I've prepared for this all . . ."

"Actually, they weren't talking about you," heaved Tashteh.

"What?" she swallowed hard.

"They said, 'The nephew of the Medicine Chief, Obed Mockko, is now slated by inside sources for the position of tribal Oracle. He will be doing his uncle's eulogy.'"

Ashneon froze. "Well, we'll see what Winay says about that. I don't think she wants an Indian who wears wiccanwear eulogizing her brother."

"The more appropriate question may be, 'what does Nuda want?' She is also Tomuck's sister and Obed Mockko is her son."

LITTLE BLUE BEINGS
ANCIENT MALI STORY

The Hombori mountains were once known as the end of the earth. There, long ago, wise little blue beings charted the comings and goings of stars, especially the travels of Sirius, that brilliant amber light in the evening sky. These little blue beings taught the mountain people that like the stars, they, too, were born of fire. They even offered them deeper secrets, which they were instructed not to share with outsiders, until they were ready for such knowledge.

Thus, the mountain people began the custom of placing a powerful Medicine Man at the entrance to their sacred cave to guard these ancient teachings until the day when the world would need them.

CHAPTER 9

PASSAGES

True, Obed was the correct choice to carry the pipe.

But why the eulogy?

Nosey little cycams swarmed Red Cedar Burial Ground like a million humming black flies, ogling the giant trees. Big Rock Boulevard had not been so lined with cars since the old casino days. That dejá vù gave some of the oldtimers a chill. Tomuck Weekum always could command a crowd. Yantuck Mountain's well-kept secret was out. Things would never be the same again.

Raw breezes, wet rot, and mildew mingled with burning white sage, its thick pillows muffling the domestic smells of cedar and sweetgrass.

Winay wore a plain blueberry sheath beneath a tightly wrapped pendleton blanket. An oblong, gray stone pendant weighed down her weedy neck like an ox yoke. Ashneon was draped in traditional black and red velvet funeral attire. Surely, there was no one better suited to simultaneously carry the colors of the living and the dead than Ashneon Quay.

The drummers chanted their loss like rolling thunder. All of the old-time Yantuck men had joined in Tomuck's sendoff. Obed Mockko entered, stage left, showcasing his dramatic six-foot six-inch frame as he swooped toward the audience. Coal-drab braids yanked at the flabby skin beside his bulging eyeballs, which rolled left-right-left in a hypnotic way. The twisted walking stick in his hand sank deeply into the soggy earth. As he leaned against a cedar tree, he swooned a little before approaching the pipe. Then came the storm of his voice, felt rather than heard, and Ashneon knew for certain that she had been upstaged.

"Tomuck Weekum now follows the path of the sun into the west," he boomed. "Star-lore tells us that his life of great wisdom will allow him to travel beyond Mother Earth and Father Sun to the starry reaches of the cosmos on his beautiful path . . ."

Obed had covered all the bases. He even convinced Tashteh to join him at the pipe. Word was out about the new Patuxet Medicine Man and Tashteh wore a crisp white shirt to his debut. The two men performed a spectacular full pipe, including Obed's special honoring for Winay and Ashneon, punctuated with grand, flowing gestures. He was flawless.

When the cameras veered in for a close-up, Obed set a sheer crystal teardrop atop Tomuck's grave. What a cycam shot. Not a local stone, and definitely not Indian-made. But who cared. Vanilla tobacco was offered to anyone wishing to bless the grave. *Vanilla tobacco!* Obed's performance omitted no optimal sensory stimuli.

Nuda hunched beside him, sporting an ancient wampum necklace over a zodiac-printed dress. Aquinnee wore a sky blue skirt beaded with leafy, trailing vines. She maintained a cryogenic pose, unaware of how stunning she looked. Beside her, Skeezucks wriggled the leather straps across the wooden bird atop his cedar flute.

As Winay motioned to the boy to step forward and present the burial song, Ashneon's stomach knotted. No one had mentioned that her little boy had received that honor. In fact, it seemed Winay had kept as much from her as possible. As his sorrow poured into the chamber, it sent forth a sharp, sweet bird whistle and Aquinnee sang along:

Jibai oke
Jibai oke
Jibai oke
Ni mus se chu

Tomuck's eyestone remained clenched inside Ashneon's soggy fist, slippery with tears and sweat. She made her way over to the grave and managed to choke out only a single, clear paragraph.

"Tomuck, we send you home to the great Earth Mother upon the path of stars. Her red-winged messengers will guide you. May you be greeted by the line of your ancestors back to the beginning. Here on the mountain you began and will continue to be. May your spirit always guide us. Journey well."

As Obed laid a woven mesh of oily crow feathers over the cremation pot, Tashteh gave Ashneon a "what the hell is that?" look. But even when Obed's rituals made no sense, his theatrics looked, sounded, and smelled terrific.

After the ceremony, when Tashteh tried to brace Obed, privately, about that hokey crow feather thing, Obed seized the opportunity to both save himself and launch a media coup.

"Here he is! Let me introduce you fine folks to Tashteh Sook, a good friend and colleague of the late Medicine Chief and who is the new Patuxet Medicine Man—a man of the ancient ways. We are honored to have him bless Tomuck's journey with his participation in this ceremony today."

A breathless cyporter stretched way up, onto tiptoes, to tap Tashteh's shoulder.

"Mr. Sook, will you be the next Oracle listing? What is your asking price? Can we scoop this?"

A burly tribal policeman motioned the pushy cyporter away. "Woman, don't you know how to behave at a funeral?" he asked.

The cyporter jolted back and forth between the three giants, soliciting amnesty but receiving none.

"This is Tomuck Weekum's day," Tashteh instructed her.

"There you are. A true man of spirit," affirmed Obed.

Catching yet another cycam opportunity, he ceremoniously

patted Tashteh's massive shoulder. "The real thing. This man's the real thing."

Obed knew that the two giants provided a spectacular cycam shot. With everyone facing them, Obed made his way over to formally embrace Winay and Ashneon, mumbling something about a splitting headache.

Now the question for Ashneon was whether to fixate on Obed's antics or the cyberazzi's attacks on Winay. An impossible choice.

Hundreds of Obed's kind had flooded the audience. Indian cotton jackets, bold and bright Andean medicine bags, southwestern desert spirit-charm animals, African trade beads, Tibetan jewelry. An exotic fruit salad of world spirituality, all secreting potent oils that made sneezing around them unavoidable. All natives from somewhere, but all abandoning their unique traditions for a generic path absent of accountability to any nagging grandmother, demanding uncle, or judgmental spirit lurking atop an ancestral mountain. It was so much easier to visit other people's mountains, where the spirits overlook you. The visitors claimed to be experts, all, in Tai chi, yoga, acupuncture, meditation, sweat lodges, pipe ceremonies and drumming. In truth, they were middling protégés whose discerning teachers remained just far enough away. There were even a few would-be tea leaf readers, none of whom could hold a candle to Nuda.

Ashneon wiped the eyestone on her sleeve. With Obed looming in front of her, she could not resist a peek through that magical stone. A gangrene shadow appeared where he stood, and beside it, a putty-colored blob, clearly signifying the hideous woman who was invading his personal space. Crisp, bleached hair hung in torn bundles over her great breasts, which spread wide apart, like misguided footballs. The book in her arms was called "Finding Your Way." That frightful sight contributed to Ashneon's ever-growing revulsion toward books. Tomuck and Tashteh had good reason to despise them.

The human menagerie had prompted most of the Indians to shrink well into the background, all except a ragged contingent of Yantuck tribal government leaders who were falling all over themselves to hop in front of any available cycam. They could have spruced up a bit more, at least put on a halfway decent aftershave for their debut before the ever-sniffing world community. Thank God most of them smelled sober, thanks to YES (Yantucks Endorsing Sobriety).

Each cleaned-up councillor craved the chance to tell the world what a good friend Tomuck Weekum had been; how they had been taught so much by him; how they would be lost without him. The real Indians softly signaled their goodbyes, crying inside, as the rain began to fall.

No matter what, this funeral was better than the ones back in the casino days, that golden age when Tribal Councillors and all pretenders to their thrones made political showings at every single tribal funeral. Those fiascos were excruciating to watch, especially for anyone who was really mourning. So few Yantucks attended tribal funerals nowadays and that was as it should be.

Squish. Squish. Squish. There was Peter, tromping through the rising puddles in his Swedish-red rain boots.

"Ready to go?" Tashteh's voice plunged from baritone to bass. Ashneon reminded him, "We have to get Winay."

"I'll go, you stay in the car," he slammed the door.

Even the most die-hard man-haters could not resist Tashteh. A sudden torrential downpour sped up the farewells. A soaked Yantuck girl splashed past. As she waved to Aquinnee and Skeezucks, her bony shoulder peeked out from beneath a baggy jacket exposing a bright and shining star.

A cluster of unfamiliar Indians appeared just as the skies

released a monsoon. Through the blurry gray sky, some of the newcomers appeared to touch the clouds. Their regalia was decorated with impressive symbols that were, for the most part, long forgotten.

Ashneon repositioned the eyestone for a better look at the latecomers, but a thud shook the hearse and jostled the eyestone onto the floor. Peter was banging his fist and pressing his dripping face against the window. "My sympathies, I'll call you." Ashneon retrieved the eyestone for re-assessment of those remarkable Indians; but they were all gone. Peter had distracted her from what was real for the last time.

"Chilly today, Win. How about some tea?" asked Ashneon.

"No thanks, birdie. Is Nuda reading today after dinner?"

"No, Win. No Sunday dinner today. Remember? Nuda is resting with Obed and the kids. How about you getting a little rest? It's been a long few days."

"Sounds good to me."

Ashneon steadied her grandmother's sharp elbows as she mounted the stairs. The old wooden steps of the Weekum House groaned as if a weighty being had been thrust upon them. Ashneon knew that if she had peaked at Winay through the eyestone, she would have spied something far grander than a scrawny, old lady in puffy yellow slippers.

Alone at last. Shrouded in an oversized robe, Ashneon nuzzled the back of Tomuck's chair beside the wood stove. Rocking, weeping, wiping her nose on her sleeve, nestling into her chair, rocking and crying some more. For the first time, nestling felt like the right thing to do. At least one of Nuda's eccentricities finally made sense.

An urgent knock un-nestled her. "It's me. Open up."

Quickly swiping her soggy cheeks, she dragged herself over

to the door to let Tashteh in. "So," she sniffed. "Was I right when I told you about my cousin, Obed Mockko?" Ashneon was slouched against the open door.

Tashteh swooped her limp body up into his arms for a great bear hug.

"He ain't nothin," Tashteh lied. "A flash in the pan. What miracles can he perform?"

"His delivery rate so far's been pretty good, I'd say. For one, he was able to instantly replace me in the position for which I trained a lifetime—without even breaking a sweat."

This time, Winay materialized, unaccompanied by even a brief staircase overture.

"Hello, children. Tomuck may be hungry later. You fix his supper, Ashneon. I'm not feeling just right," Winay whispered.

Tashteh looked on helplessly, as Ashneon's eyes dissolved into turbulent turquoise seas.

"Don't worry about anything, Win. Go back and finish your rest. I'll bring you some saltines and tea," Ashneon said.

The old Medicine Woman allowed the young Medicine Man to escort her back up to her room. As they walked, the wily steps creaked, moaned and lamented the human condition. The house was up to its old tricks again.

"I can stay awhile," reassured Tashteh.

"No. Thanks anyway. Really. Head on back to your own territory. I have a trip to make this evening. Some folks I need to try and talk to."

Tashteh smoothed her swollen, soggy cheek, then retreated back down the mountain. The eyestone was lying on the windowsill and Ashneon stole a glimpse of him before he fell out of sight; but all she saw were starry flecks of light.

CHAPTER 10
HIGHER UP

Come spring, Ashneon regularly fled the Weekum House for the sanctuary of the museum. The mice and spiders knew the truth: the museum was really just woods in disguise. They lived there just as anywhere else outdoors. That was why Tomuck had slept there so often; he could not separate himself from the trees and a bed at the museum meant that he did not have to.

The cheerful morning songbirds instilled Ashneon with enough courage to enter the gloomy bedroom, where Winay's waxy features clashed mightily against the sunny, daisy swirl of her pillowcase.

"Weekwasun Winay!"

"Good morning to you too, birdie. I guess you'll need to be on deck again today. It's kind of chilly. There won't be too many visitors, and it seems like I am not mending as well as I had hoped."

Winay had elevated excuses to an art form. It was getting harder and harder to remember who and what she had once been.

The old woman continued, "oh, you'll be glad to know Peter called and said he is coming by."

"Did he say when?" Ashneon stifled a groan.

"He's on his way over right now."

"I'm headed up the path, then."

Armed with a potent mug of Columbian cawhee, Ashneon marched up the trail. On the way into the museum, she poked her nose into the collection basket. Tomuck's wooden Indian head nickel still rattled at the bottom. Another treasure to protect. She tucked it away up on a high shelf right beside that irritating wooden doll all dressed in green.

Seeing that nickel had made her chest ache. He could not really be gone. A bold flash of amber and gold light appeared. Solar storms, just as Tomuck used to described them, "Nature's Grand Fireworks."

What would Tomuck say about those mighty bursts?

"He would say they mean Father Sun is dying," answered a familiar voice.

"Tomuck? Oh Tomuck!"

"Thanks for calling me, Medicine Girl."

"But I had been calling you all winter and I still can't see you! Oh, I'm so glad you're back! At least to talk to. I've missed you so! I had nearly given up on visiting you. Where are you anyway? Wha—What did you mean about Father Sun dying?"

"Ain't nothing. Sun could hang on this way a couple more million years before he goes for good. But he is dying. Sputtering, erupting, petering out. Fire and light signal life or death. For some to be born, the universe must eliminate others. In this case, death for ol' Father Sun means life for who knows what. I understand such things directly now."

"Did you journey well?"

"Journey was great. Nothing to fear as far as that goes. All kinds of oldtimers brought me on through. But it seems I didn't go too far. This museum appears to be my primary resting space in the great hereafter, at least for the time being."

His voice came from nowhere in particular and Ashneon was unsure whether she was actually hearing him with her ears.

"Winay isn't doing well."

"So it would seem," he replied.

"Will she snap out of it?"

"Who knows. Uh Oh! Your boy Peter is here. Time to do your duty with the living. We'll talk later. Don't you worry, I'm not going anywhere. That's why you couldn't find me on the other side; there's still too much of me right here."

The door grumbled as it opened.

"Ashneon?" Peter poked his head in.

The hairs on her arm shot up straight. But, for the first time, her breathing was fine.

Hey, I've missed you," he confessed, offering a shaky open hand. Ashneon backed away and Peter noticed that her eyes had deepened to a rich teal. Nonetheless, he blundered ahead. "I brought you some stuff for your research on rattles. That is, if you're ready. I mean, I can come back another time if you'd rather not."

A hysterical chorus of giggles rippled through the airwaves; but Peter refused to hear them. He wiggled an index finger in and out of each ear, attempting to ferret out the anomaly.

"I'm sorry. I should have known this would be too soon. I'll come back later," he apologized.

"Come here," she commanded. "You want to know about rattles, Peter? Here. Hold this and tell me what you can. Take it."

The turtle's shell pulsated, its venom coursing through his veins.

"Ouch! What? Did I say something wrong? I can come back another time."

"Tell me about this rattle," she insisted. "Let's see how well your hands can read."

Peter stuttered, "well, from what I found in the archive, it is probably seventeenth-century, a box turtle, cedar handle. I think there may even be some rare Munsee Wolf beans inside. It must have been used in an important ceremony."

"Let me see it," she commanded.

Ashneon grasped the rattle like a scepter and focused her mental muscles. The cedar handle melted into her hand as she spoke:

I am Noquay of the time when our people saw little of white men. This turtle was an old one even then. His cranberry eyes had dulled but his nose still turned proudly toward the sky and his neck could extend as far as any. In life, few things drove him to the safety of his shell. He had little fear because his memory held the past and future at all times. He guided me for many years and I called him little grandfather—Cocheesee.

When he passed on at a great age, I carved this handle for him from a cedar tree struck down by lightning and filled his shell with muskerzeet beans. Then I brought him to the Dark Dance. There, we walked the circle together, he and I beneath the stars, turning slowly to the rhythm of the swirling earth beneath and the whirling sky above. Through my moccasins, I felt Mother Earth's stiff bones and rushing blood. Through Cocheesee, I felt the fiery warmth of both her hot belly and the blazing stars. Cocheesee, the universe, and I, we three walked as one. As Lead Rattle, the others answered him. Heartbeats rang out from the tribal drummers, joining the rush of blood, bone, and fire, 'til dance became flesh; Cocheesee's shell was full and alive again in my hand. Drumbeats in three, three, three. Powerful magic, greater than other ceremonies before. Cocheesee honored my people and his medicine drew powerful spirits to our prayers.

For many years after that, we danced together, but that first dance was the burning dance of life, of he and I, Mother Earth and Father Sky, joined in the ceremony of birth into the universe. Later, my great grandson, Weetop, took my place bringing in the Dark Dance. Weetop will now speak . . .

I am Weetop. In my day, many museums wanted to acquire Cocheesee, but he was too much for them to handle. When I met Winay Weekum, she was only a girl and I was her teacher. But I knew Cocheesee had found a home. I told her that this rattle had passed its time and needed a protected place to rest, surrounded by others of its kind. So Winay Weekum brought Cocheesee here, where he became the eldest of the rattles. I watch over him, because one day, the Medicine People of Yantuck Mountain will need Cocheesee for the ultimate cere-mony, the ceremony that finishes one world and begins another. NiYaYo.

Peter was sucking desperately hard on his respiratory inhaler, his face drained of all color, but for a single constellation of freck-les upon each cheek.

"What was that, Ashneon?" he wheezed.

"*That* was the reality I almost missed by thinking knowledge came from books. Now I read objects and they speak volumes."

"So now you agree with Tomuck, about books being bad?" he whined.

It was all suddenly crystal clear. Peter was glued to a cheap lawn chair outside the ropes at the Great Pow Wow of Life while Ashneon stood center circle, a proud competition dance final-ist, boasting a shiny new jingle dress.

"All the journal articles in the world can never capture the lessons of Tomuck Weekum, or even one object at this museum," she explained. "Each artifact's story holds multiple layers. Books are so primitive. College has lost its luster for me. I'm wondering how come somebody had to die for me to see what was right in front of me. From now on, I'll be busy filling in for Winay and Tomuck at our folksy little museum and com-pletely neglecting our groundbreaking scholarly research."

"Okay, okay. You've made your point," he puffed.

Static charges halted his roving hand before it contacted

her shoulder. That was it. Peter needed to retreat back to his own world quickly, before his solid, steady life turned to jello. He strode back out the door boldly, as white men often do when making a last stand, then scampered lickety-split down the mountain. Ashneon held up the eyestone and peered thru it in his direction, but there was nothing there.

"Tomuck?" called Ashneon.

"Yes."

"Now I know why you spent so much time up here at night."

"You are welcome to use the room in back. It's your room now. I always keep spare linens in the closet."

"I think I'll take you up on that," she smiled.

Making up her bed, Ashneon was nowhere near lonely. A lively cricket chirped at her feet and a grape vine tickled her arm. A mask on the wall heaved a restful sigh. The museum was terribly crowded. But Ashneon knew she was surrounded by real teachers, genuine friends, and true Oracles.

CHAPTER 11
NEW LIGHTERS CLIMB

Mountain crows were renowned for their lack of manners. No less offensive were the droning coos of the morning doves. But even the combined sunrise assault of the entire winged kingdom hardly penetrated the plaster walls, insulated windows, and solid cherry doors of the Weekum House.

Up at the museum, however, things were quite different. There, the buzzes and hums of flies and bees, chittering squirrels, chirping birds, and squealing woodchucks orchestrated a cacophony that sometimes knocked Ashneon right out of bed in the morning. Still, if she listened very carefully and peeled back the stentorian layers, way down deep she could hear the hushed chatter of the artifacts.

Ashneon yawned and propped an elbow onto her pillow. "Tomuck?"

"Right here. A bit noisy some mornings isn't it? Quite the symphony. Well, looks like there's no time for us to converse today. You've got another big day ahead. Unwelcome visitors are coming—and soon."

"Oh, you mean Obed. Not to worry. I've been expecting him," she stiffened.

"No, it's not any of our folks. Definitely incidentals."

"Whoever it is, I'll be ready for them. By the way, can you please talk to Winay? Get her to snap out of her haze and help me?"

"You give it another try first," replied Tomuck.

That was Ashneon's cue to descend to the dreadful house. These days, each trip down the mountain felt like an agonizing fall from grace.

The once-proud matriarch sagged beside the kitchen table like a poster child for reservation reform.

"Winay. Winay! Excuse me." She snapped her fingers. "Tomuck says we're expecting important visitors today and they're not relatives. You up to it?"

"No, birdie, I think I better lie low a little longer, just to be sure."

"Tomuck says that's not a good idea. He's coming to speak to you today," Ashneon prodded.

"Oh, stop it now. Tomuck's passed on." The old woman's eyelids sank to half mast, and her body remained as stiff as a corn husk doll.

"Well, suit yourself. I know he wants to tell you something," insisted Ashneon.

Winay came to life a bit, briefly, as a bus with a glittering purple pentagram roared by. The folks Tomuck had warned about, no doubt—all coming to see Winay at the worst possible time.

The passengers floated out the door behind their leader, a lanky woman with copper tipped hair. Hammered copper snakes adorned her upper arms. She sure knew how to attract an Indian's attention. At first glance, the entourage resembled a stray European musical group. But foreign entertainers never came to the mountain anymore, not since the casino closed.

As the group leader rapped on the Weekum house front door, she fought the breezes billowing up her diaphanous skirt.

"Aquay. Greetings," Ashneon said.

The glamorous stranger's eye makeup shifted through a holographic spectrum, allowing each turn of the head to spawn a fresh deception.

"Oh I am so honored to meet you, Miss Quay. I am West Wind Monroe and this is my New Light group." Ashneon struggled not to grimace as the visitor heaved breathily into each word. "I am a friend of your cousin Obed. He speaks so highly of you and your grandmother. Is there any chance at all that we might pay our respects to the great lady?"

Her wide, pleading eyes nearly burst out of their sockets. West delicately covered her mouth with quavering fingertips and deliberately lowered her voice, "Or is it best to simply leave off this gift?"

She continued to strum her peculiar musical instrument while prattling on about Ashneon's quaint beads and retro house decor. The instrument fastened to West's shoulder resembled a miniature clarsach harp. When Ashneon asked about it, the visitor explained that it was a Rhythmear, an ingenious device that detected rhythms in group interaction then replicated appropriate instrumental selections designed to enhance the group's mood—thus bolstering the energy of dialogue.

Winay's limp, gray form staggered in during the explanation.

"Oh, I am overwhelmed," West squealed. "How wonderful to meet you, Ms. Weekum. Don't you look well!"

"Would you like to come in?" insisted Winay, instantly perkier and colorized. "That was a lovely melody that you, um, joined with your speech."

"Oh, I am so pleased that you like it."

The hypnotic, sympathetic tones lilted on.

"Now, just a moment, let me play something new." West was wiggling to adjust her clingy skirt again. "I wrote this particular healing melody just for you. Oh, but we couldn't possibly stay. I know you are still suffering from your great loss."

"Don't be silly. I would love to hear more," countered Winay. "You mustn't leave. We've been moping around here long enough. And please, have your friend come in too." Winay was peering past West at the stunning, as-yet-unintroduced male just outside the door.

"Please, sir, come in and join us."

The old woman spiked an eager eyebrow as he entered. That curious instrument seemed to have livened her up.

She waved him in. "I may not be up to full strength but I'll sit a minute with you young folks. Then my granddaughter, Ashneon, will show you around the museum."

"You are so gracious in person, Ms. Weekum. I just can't believe this blessing," gushed West, playing bold tones of amazement.

West's skulking companion drew forward and the screen door snapped shut across his outstretched fingers. No one noticed the house's assault.

"Dr. Foxon Arber," West introduced him with a slight jiggle. "This is Winay Weekum, the Oracle, and her granddaughter, Ashneon Quay."

Ashneon winced.

Foxon shook back his California mane to reveal eyes the color of a wet beach. Winay could not help but stare. His throbbing fingers presented her with a smooth chamois pouch, beaded in succulent shades of honeydew and cantaloupe, as a trumpet fanfare spewed forth from the Rhythmear.

"I made this just for you," he crooned.

West placed a hand on her heart and crinkled her forehead in an absurd way.

"Their auras together, so moving, so much good white energy," West said. "Oh, thank you, Ashneon, for letting us share this moment."

"I have something for you as well, Ms. Quay," Foxon turned abruptly and grazed Ashneon's throat with a vanilla scented peacock feather. "I know you love birds," he confided.

Ashneon attempted to choke out a thank you, but something swallowed her words. It was uncomfortable enough to have been researched, never mind by some New Light Adonis.

"Take these nice folks up to the museum, while I get a little rest," directed Winay with a smirk.

Foxon motioned down to the group to come along and West elevated her tempo to a somewhat peppier uphill marching beat. Even so, her sandy-haired followers did not pick up the pace, but, rather, appeared to ooze up the mountain like honey.

At the summit in front of the museum their hive was instantly reduced to a collection of helpless, disconnected drones. West dropped the Rhythm Ear onto an oak bench and began to hyperventilate. The spirit of Yantuck Mountain was too much for them.

"When you're up to it, you can come right this way," beckoned Ashneon smugly.

They would get nothing beyond the usual tour. They were takers, drainers, spiritual succubi. As they wandered through the museum, they bypassed all the magnificent and weighty objects; those artifacts knew how and when to hide. Only Tomuck's most trivial mementos sparked their interest: photographs of the Chief with various governors, commemorative Indian coins, a state legislative proclamation for "Yantuck Indian Day." All garbage.

"Ashneon you have so many wonderfully special things. They carry such good energy. We can learn so much from one another."

Next came the predictable New Light hug. West pierced Ashneon with her formidable chest and slithered artful fingertips gently up and down her spine.

"It must have been such an honor, growing up with Tomuck and Winay and the Master," cooed West.

That last word froze Ashneon stiff.

Foxon tore in like a bloodhound, "West, where are our manners? I'm so sorry, Ashneon. We who have come to know the great abilities and training of your cousin Obed refer to him, respectfully, as 'the Master.' No disrespect to yourself, or the Great Winay, intended of course."

"So you are planning to—" Ashneon began for them.

"Yes, you see, of course," said Foxon. "We are here to help the Ma . . . , uh, Obed assume his rightful place as male Oracle. We do not in any way wish to alter your path, following in Winay's footsteps as female Oracle."

"We call them Medicine People." Ashneon corrected.

Foxon fluttered his dreamy eyes, "Of course you do, my dear." He clasped her hands, "Ashneon, we understand you are quite the little scholar."

West interjected. "Oh, my, yes! You will appreciate that Foxon here knows seventeen languages, all associated with the greatest ancient religious texts Aramaic, Sanskrit, Hindi, Tibetan, Mayan. Oh, just all of them. You and he can talk books. It will be great fun for you to get to know one another."

Foxon had obviously gotten to know plenty of women that way already. Surely he was one of those who had opted for bio-inoculations against STDs. Even a few Yantuck men had gone that route. But not Tashteh. Not ever.

Books were Foxon's standard bait, but they would never hook Ashneon, since they had recently become her Nemesis. Book storage places existed in boxes under nearly every museum exhibit. Tomuck sometimes called Winay "Ms. Tucker," because she tucked books into every imaginable nook and cranny. But Ashneon knew exactly where the enemy was hiding.

The battle was on. The object of the operation was to search and destroy. Inside the glass exhibit cases stood true comrades, armed and ready to obliterate the designated target. The days of the musty round-spined invaders were numbered.

CHAPTER 12
SILENCE

Tashteh's offer of a spring road trip on Ye Olde Patuxet Trail was a blessing. Although recently transformed into the area's main highway, it remained the ancient thoroughfare. Inches below the surface lay an archaeological paradise of snowflake obsidian, grassy chert, quahog disks, and pony beads. Kicked about and carted along from God knows where, these hidden treasures continued to be felt.

It was seventy-five degrees, but the Patuxet Medicine Man cranked up the heat in the truck; he loathed spring dampness, said it made him bone-wet. Tashteh's chilly condition frequently provoked skirmishes, since Ashneon's was a perpetual inferno.

Soon after crossing the river, Tashteh began to fidget with the rearview mirror, the cy controls, and his shirt collar.

"Do you sense an unnatural quiet?" he finally asked.

The tremor in his voice startled her.

"Yes," she replied. "It's like when I go between worlds, a 'netherworldliness.'"

"Not good, Ashneon. This is the fallout of some sort of project."

"Tashteh, why did we decide to go on this trip?"

"I guess I thought you needed a break. But why did we pick right now?"

"I'll call Winay and see if everything is all right."

"Hi, Winay. Yes it's . . . What? Who is with you? Why? When did they get there? What exactly did they say? You told them what? I'll be right there."

The tendons in Ashneon's neck were drawn taught, like an overstrung bow about to snap.

Nuda was perched on the Weekum House front steps, blowing great aromatic clouds from a chalky kaolin pipe.

"You just missed them," she puffed, pulling herself halfway up through the murky swells. These days, halfway up was the best she could do under any circumstances.

"I didn't know," Nuda apologized, waving goodbye to Tashteh. "Don't know how come I know everything else 'cept what fool thing my own son's gonna do. I never could figure men. I had a bad blind spot when it came to his father and the same's true with the son. I'm sorry, girl."

"Nuda, how much did Winay grant him?" Ashneon swallowed.

"Too much. He's got the full medicine nod. She told him he could start taking on some of Tomuck's duties right away, and he had three witnesses. I wouldn't be surprised if New Light Corporation is offering his Oracle stock options online right this very minute."

"Has it been quiet like this here all day?" probed Ashneon.

"You know—Why yes, now that you mention it. Ashneon! Oh no! I'm ashamed I didn't notice it earlier. Dark magic is afoot here. No doubt about that."

"Whose work is it, do you suppose?" asked Ashneon.

"Well, my guess would be one of Obed's minions. They seem to be the low-end, Wiccan type. You know, fools that play with black forces and do projects. Not members of any respectable coven." Nuda concluded with a hearty sniff.

"Who was with him? West Wind?" asked Ashneon.

"Yes, her, but there were quite a few others too. All look the same to me. Could have been any one of 'em." Nuda dropped back down firmly and began to nestle. "He says he wants to move in permanently with me and the twins, you know. I can't very well deny him. This is his home and I can't keep him away from his own children. Some of that crowd are over my house right now—hence the reason I am sitting out here. Quite a few of 'em are Europeans, you know. Must've exhausted the domestic seer market. They make me sick. I used the back staircase once already today, to slip away and wouldn't you know it, there was Obed, right there, poking around them back stairs. I told him it was a private area, off limits to visitors and he needn't be using them, neither. He mumbled something about havin' to visit Danugun on them stairs." Nuda began to stutter, "L-l-looking for s-s-sympathy, no doubt. D-didn't get n-none from me!"

Those back stairs led to more than Nuda would ever tell. When she was younger, Ashneon once dreamt that she flew down them. When she told Nuda about it, the old lady had spiked a quivering eyebrow.

Nuda's back staircase had been built by Danugun Mockko's father, Fin Ohgma: An Irishman of such unnatural strength and size, he had easily beaten down the mightiest Yantuck men vying for the hand of Danugan's mother, Ponemah. Tomuck loved big Fin so much, he often called him Green Medicine. After all, Tomuck said, "Real Medicine People are the same everywhere."

Ohgma hailed from Great Blasket Island in western Ireland, where he had been raised by his mother, Maeve, a traditional healer who named her fourteen-pound newborn son after the ancient hero Fin McCool. She faithfully instructed young Fin in the old ways, forever pestering him about offerings to Danu, the ancient spirit of earth and water. Fin claimed that when he was a teenager, he had only just placed a flask of whiskey atop Danu's shrine when a vision of his future bride, a young Yantuck Indian woman, rose above the cliffs, beckoning him to fetch her from across the Atlantic sea. At that moment, Fin swore to Danu that if he ever won the love of that glorious woman, their child would honor her name.

Big Fin soon discovered the woman in his vision to be sixteen-year-old Ponemah Wahsus. The happy couple shared only five magical years before Ponemah was called to cross over. Fin kept going for his daughter, Danugun's, sake. But shortly after her twenty-first birthday, Danugun joined her mother on the other side. That was when Fin took to peering intently across the Atlantic ocean each sunrise, as if he could surely see Ireland if he squinted hard enough.

The day Fin finished painting Nuda's back staircase a light seagull gray was the day that the old man disappeared for good. Tomuck swore that "Fin Ohgma just raised up his arms and flew back home across the Atlantic sea." But Winay insisted that "he probably just drowned in a bottle of whiskey right on shore."

Either way, Fin Ohgma left his mark on Yantuck Mountain. No other Yantuck house had anything like the Mockko family back stairs. Each step was outfitted with an unsettling image, except for the center landing where Ohgma had carved a tranquil, soaring wren. The steep incline of those steps was inspired by Ohgma's sheer native cliffs. However, Fin knew that the Yantuck were prone to vertigo, so he designed a broad midway that made it impossible to fall too far.

The oddest thing about those gray stairs was the funny clicking sound your feet made when you tripped up and down them, like you were step dancing in tap shoes. Aquinnee and Skeezucks loved the rhythms they could produce by scampering up and down, faster and faster, covering them from top to bottom with happy scuff marks.

Nuda did not let just anyone use that back staircase. She insisted it belonged to Aquinnee and Skeezucks. Their grandfather had built it for them. Period.

"One lucky thing," confided Nuda. "I think Obed's groupies

have finally given up on me. Ever since I told them I only read teacups for Indian Women, they been looking at me like I'm suffering from some sort of psychic disability."

"Well Nuda, we'll see about all the supposed magic, medicine and miracles of these New Lighters tomorrow, when Obed and his friends face the Yantuck people and the mountain head on."

CHAPTER 13

MIRACLE

Franticly fluttering eyes, still, even breath, slightly jolting head. At precisely eleven fifty-seven P.M., Ashneon dreamed of a long-legged woman with ebony ringlets and shamrock eyes.

"Danugan!" exclaimed Ashneon. "I was wondering how I could get out of this dream until now. I thought you might be some night terror or something. It's great to see you!"

"I am sorry about the approach, Ashneon. I know that dreams are a funny realm for you. But I tried other methods to get through to you from the other side these last few days. However, you blocked anything to do with Obed, and that unfortunately includes me! When you passed by my headstone yesterday, you ignored me completely. I was tugging at you and you didn't even flinch."

"But Danugun, I have tried to talk to Obed. I told him that if he would just believe in the mountain, he might gain some of the same powers I have and be able to talk to you. But maybe, deep down, the whole subject of you is too painful for him."

"An eternity of being cut off from him is too painful for me, Ash. Besides, he and I have ongoing business—you know—about the twins. And what is he thinking, dabbling in projects? How could he forget what happened to me, or your parents?"

"What do you mean?"

Her image dimmed to a faint silhouette. That was obviously the wrong topic.

"Never mind that," Ashneon said. "Obed will exercise any power in this universe that claims to bring you back. He knows our medicine can't upset the balance. So, that makes him vulnerable to the medicine of far-off places with far-flung claims.

I've always loved you, Danugun. You were my best friend. You made Obed whole. What can I do now to help you both?"

"When you awaken, you will know."

Blazing sunbeams pronounced her tardiness. The critters had been squawking for hours. Danugun had said this would be a big day, which meant that being late could prove dangerous. Yesterday's clothes and a fast braid would have to do.

"Winay, I'm going over to Nuda's for a bit."

No response.

Tomuck had built the stone foot path between his sisters' houses: a walking mosaic of rust, teal, taupe, and ashen slates. The urge to skip across those stones was irresistible. Nuda's yard, at the other end, was packed with a slew of junker cars. There was no driveway, so everyone parked in piles rather than rows.

Ashneon carefully hopped up the crumbling front steps. The Mockko house had been homeless for a very long time now. No one had cared for it since Muggs died. Nuda always acted as though she were expecting Muggs to burst in at any moment, so she could nag him about catching up on those neglected chores.

From outside, the scrappy yelling was audible only in selective spurts of "you asshole!" and "let him finish!" Inside, Ryan Tianu had commandeered center stage.

"Obed Mockko," Ryan pointed upward at him with a stiff arm, as if casting a curse. "When's the last time you stood for your people? You know what happened after Big Rock went under. You were there. You saw what our people did to one another," he growled. "You love to criticize me, but when did you ever stand up for your people? And now you want to replace Medicine Chief Tomuck Weekum. Hah!"

He strutted toward the door, then flashed a hot little finger back up at Obed. "You think we'll all just sit back and let you be anointed some kind of Greek god. We don't need any New Light here. We have plenty of our own old light!" He pointed at Ashneon. "We have real medicine here. Obed, you say you'll save your people? How? By what kind of fool's medicine? Oh, that's right. Your father tried that already. Remind me again what happened there!"

Ashneon felt a polar chill creep up her spine. Aquinnee kicked Skeezucks' foot.

Obed yelled, "that's enough, Tianu. Leave my father out of this. He wasn't the only one to blame for . . . I needed those travels to other people and places to expand on what little I was taught here. You understand that, don't you Ashneon?"

Something swallowed her reply. In fact, no one, but Obed, was able to utter a sound. Having spied West scrunched over a stubby gray candle in the kitchen performing some sort of hocus pocus, Ashneon dashed over to toss the smouldering paraphernalia into the sink. After that, the energy shifted.

"Obed, Do you dabble in European projects?" Ashneon demanded.

"I pull together any power at my disposal to bring forth great energy and love," he replied.

"I'll take that as a yes. Will you face the judgment of your ancestors for encouraging poorly-wrought—not to mention alien to this soil—Wiccan medicine for ill purposes here on Yantuck Mountain?" she insisted.

"I am not ashamed of any medicine belonging to the elementals of this Earth. Ashneon, you're well-read enough not to be so provincial. I know you don't really believe the medicine of others has any less value than our own. You don't think the Great Creator of this universe made Medicine People only on Yantuck Mountain, do you?"

"Obed, I agree that real Medicine People are the same

everywhere. But they do not all derive their medicine from the same places. Nor are they all real. This mountain is your home and you never gave it a chance. You don't even know what this place really is. And I've about had enough of your brand of medicine now that I've seen that you allow your followers to use projects to help you get your way!"

"Please, my dear," Foxon stepped forward, lowering his eyes. "You must understand the Master's studies were inspired by teachings gleaned from the greatest avatars of today's world. He has studied hundreds of elemental beings, read all the ancient texts available, even witnessed amazing miracles in far off regions. Yet we must all remember that he began his great quest quite simply: he just wanted to find a way to speak to his late wife. Surely you can understand that need."

The Indians in the room snickered with glee, and Foxon immediately regretted his mistake.

"Show 'em how its done Ashneon Quay," boomed Ryan Tianu. "I've had enough of those who think they know medicine cuz they once had tea with the Dalai Lama."

All eyes fell on Ashneon.

"For those of you who are friends of Obed and don't know me, I am his cousin, Ashneon Quay. I grew up in the Weekum house, right over there, and I—regularly visit the dead."

"Go get 'em, Ashneon." Rattles began to shake, buoyed up by hand drums and multiple war whoops. The room was suddenly completely alive with vibrating chairs, floor, and ceiling.

"I, too, have lost people whom I loved very much. Obed's late wife, Danugun, was my dear friend. My own parents died right after I was born."

"And whose fault was that?" Ryan snarled at Obed.

Ashneon continued grittily. "By staying here on the mountain, I found my answers. Not by running away. I may be able to show Obed how to talk to his wife, Danugun, if he'll let me.

But I cannot show him how to meddle with people's thoughts and desires using dark, foreign medicine or how to bring his wife back to life for good. That sort of magic won't work on this mountain."

Foxon smirked. "I appreciate your traditional, conservative views. But Obed has far surpassed the limitations of your fundamentalist, indigenous medicine. I know you believe you speak to the dead. But that may be all it is, my dear—just a belief."

The sandy-haired Adonis had finally ripped off his mask.

"Go ahead Ashneon!" Ryan egged her on.

"All right. Who will walk with me to Danugun Mockko's grave to listen to what she has to say?"

"I see no point," intoned Foxon. "You can say she told you whatever you want. We have no way to verify your story."

"I will go," said Obed, shooting Foxon a razor glance.

"Yes, Master," bowed Foxon. "As you wish."

Ashneon led the apostles past the sea of potholes, formerly known as Big Rock Boulevard, toward Red Cedar Burial Ground. A row of vaulted white birch trees led to the three acres of headstones on the high banks of the Quinnepaug river.

Danugun Mockko's headstone caught the last glint of a squash blossom sunset. Aquinnee and Skeezucks fought back tears. As soon as Ashneon touched the glistening granite, Obed took Skeesucks's hand, it was then that the falling sensation hit her. It was an especially long fall for Ashneon, followed, briefly, by the usual whistling, then an eerie stillness that lasted far too long.

Winay had warned her never to dawdle in the Spirit World when things remained all-too silent like that, something about the possibility of being trapped in the in-between. Ashneon hated to leave so soon, as the thought of making excuses to Foxon was sickening. Nonetheless, she had to head straight back.

Upon re-emerging into the land of the living, she gasped to find spectators lying at her feet. Farther down the riverbank, Obed appeared to be searching the Quinnepaug River for absolution, his bloodless lips tightly pursed in a frozen kiss. Beside him, Skeezucks stood slack-jawed beside a motley contingent of Obed's followers, murmuring like a swarm of hornets.

Only Aquinnee acknowledged Ashneon's return by running over to kiss her.

"Tawbut nee, oh thank you. I had always dreamed this, my greatest wish! To see my mother again and touch her—even for one minute! She was everything I dreamed. Oh Ashneon, Ashneon it was wonderful. Skeezucks can't even speak, he misses her so, even though he never admitted it. So have I, of course, but I always had you and you are magic—truly magic! I don't think anyone believes what they just saw except me and Skeezucks. Dad's upset. But a good upset. Seeing my mother was like a dream, Ashneon, a beautiful dream. Forget those stupid New Light Oracles. You are the truly amazing one!"

Ashneon closed her eyes and threw her arms around the girl's shoulders. "No, not really," she whispered.

CHAPTER 14
EYE OF STONE

Y OUNG MEDICINE WOMAN RAISES THE DEAD. The Miracle of Yantuck Mountain had thus been reduced to a supermarket tabloid.

Foxon wore a lily white suit, shirt and tie to the press conference. No one had ever seen him wear a tie before.

"A trumped-up business ploy," he declared, rubbing a polished rose quartz stone between his thumb and forefinger. "That's all this nonsense really is. Those mountain people covet the Master's contract with New Light Corporation, pure and simple. Imagine them staging that phony resurrection. What a cruel hoax! I won't go so far as to agree with the rumors that Ashneon Quay actually tried to sabotage the Master's Oracle listing in order to obtain her own. But, well . . ." he hesitated, cast his eyes downward, and shook his head, "I cannot deny that claim either."

The audience was jam-packed with the faithful. Word of Danugun's resurrection had spread like wildfire through the New Light community.

"This whole thing has been blown out of proportion. The light will expose the truth, just as it always does." Foxon went on, "Let us harbor no ill will against anyone. All human beings are drawn to the light. Sometimes, if the light is very bright, it blinds those closest to it. Let us therefore pray for the family of Tomuck Weekum, his sisters, nieces, nephews and, most especially, his young Ashneon Quay."

Foxon spread lies like butter. The irony was that he and his New Light buddies professed to want nothing more than a miracle, and having witnessed a whopper, instantly dismissed it. No bard rejoiced in song, no noble warrior proffered treasure for the glorious deed. Instead, they stoned and mocked the hero like a common criminal, in keeping with western religious tradition.

The Indians were not much better. They loved Ashneon for about a minute and a half. Then they went back to denouncing her as delusional. The other word being tossed around the tribe was "grandstanding." Many concurred with Foxon: Ashneon put on her sideshow for money, to capture a prime Oracle position.

Indians loved to corroborate the enemy's lies.

Still, the incident preoccupied people's minds enough for Foxon to call in reinforcements. He invited Earthbeats (a chart-topping women's drumming group) to the Mockko house to beat their bongos in support of their Oracle. This gender-bending atrocity combined men's hunting rhythms with women's blanket dances, thus ultimately rousing Winay out of her stupor. The old woman was suddenly well enough to call up her sister Nuda and gripe.

"So I see you have finally lost your mind. Letting that sacrilege into your home! What Tomuck would say about women drumming and singing men's songs. What he would say! I'll bet they even hold sweats with the men and carry pipes!

It was nervy for Winay to have assailed Nuda about losing *her* mind. But Nuda restrained herself from reminding Winay about her own recent mental stumblings.

In spite of the all-pervasive family insanity, Ashneon pressed on with museum tours in the damp but lively building where Tomuck's voice continued to ring out from everywhere.

Observe. Concentrate. Remember. She stared into the eye-stone and continued to mutter that pesky limerick:

There once was a stone with an eye
Through which all chosen spirits could spy
Without effort or task

It could rip any mask
Be it ruse, trick, deception, or lie.

What was it really all about? And where did it come from?

"Study the in-betweens," Tomuck always said. "The shades of gray, the images caught in the corner of the eye; pull off the mask—uncover the real medicine, the unlimited possibilities."

Medicine was such a serious, all-consuming and complex family business. Tashteh knew that, too. The Patuxet were having a big time about his recent appointment as Medicine Man. No one had ever seen so many installation / confirmation / affirmation ceremonies for one position. It was obvious that the hub-bub was just a ploy to hook him up with one of his own women, before that crazy Yantuck gal (who talks to the dead) polluted his line. The prince needed a princess, and she had better hail from his native land.

Ashneon knew that the situation was as it should be and therefore accepted every excuse for his absence, even though a different pathway to her heart closed with each and every one.

"Ashneon, I'm sorry I can't go with you to the social. There's a fire for me at the Longhouse today." "Ashneon, I have to perform a pipe today, so we'll need to reschedule our trip."

He was Patuxet public property. The women of his Tribe owned him whether she liked it or not—especially Wunneah Tatoon. Wunneah was about the same age as Ashneon but more interested in making Indian babies than talking to the dead. Wunneah wanted a Patuxet husband with good bloodlines and there was no denying that she would make a perfect wife for Tashteh. Wunneah was simply the better choice—a womanly woman who could reduce his load and replicate the right blood quantum for the next generation. Meanwhile, Ashneon had never done well at simply being a woman. It was neither her primary function nor even one of her top ten. Of course, that did not stop her blood from boiling at the mention of Wunneah's name.

Winay's medicine mask hung from a peg board in the center of the museum beside the turtle rattle. Ashneon carefully removed it and slipped the leather straps around her ears.

Watch out for anything carved from the spirit of a living tree. Tomuck was muttering again.

The wooden face locked into her own. Shrink-fit. Like a second skin. Instantly, everything shifted and she was fathoms beneath the ocean staring at two ancient sea turtles swimming toward her. Nothing moved except their eyes, spinning rainbow prisms in which Ashneon glimpsed the fatal reflection of her own eyes and fiercely tore off the mask. There, standing right in front of her, were Nuda and Winay.

Ashneon's face lit up. "Winay, you came up!"

"Thought you needed some help," said Winay. "Looks like we were wrong." Winay picked up the mask. "I see that you have learned some things in my absence. Seems you've neglected your book research a bit, though. Well, I suppose it's time I introduced you to some of the other folks up here who you may not have met yet."

A wind rushed into the room, as if hundreds of doors had suddenly blown open. Winay inhaled deeply, drinking in the fresh breeze like it was the fountain of youth.

"Oh, birdie, where to begin, where to begin? Ah! Here we are. This offering basket for your friend Bawba carries the voices of many women, but most especially one named Mossuck." The old woman twittered. "One of his favorites."

She continued to lecture. "See how the basket is marked with the ancient Beacher language. Trouble is, that language can only be read by Mossuck; it can only be learned in dreams, and even then, only if she decides to teach you. So, the linguists had to claim this writing was a fraud. I heard about this basket and requested she be sent here years ago. See how her story reads, round and round in a spiral not left to right or right to left. No lines. You know academics: anything too complicated for them to glean must be a hoax. Among these objects, you will find there is always at least one special teacher for everyone."

"Like that growling bear club of Tomuck's?" asked Ashneon.

"Oh, yes indeed! You understand some of this quite well, already, don't you? And this chair here, she was Nuda's teacher. Her name is Pually. The stories she tells stretch back to the beginning of time and forward to the end. When she was alive, Pually was a terrific fortune-teller, like Nuda. They often consult with one another about issues in the tasseography profession. That's all fortune-telling is, you know—finding a way to read stories from the future."

"Aren't there any men up here Winay?"

"Yes, but as you know," Winay's eyes shifted furtively, "your old grandmother never managed well with men, especially your grandfather." She coughed and sputtered a moment. "You on the other hand, you may have better luck. Perhaps times have changed. How many dead men have you spoken to?"

"Quite a few. Of course I speak to Tomuck—who inhabits these walls—and the men in the turtle shell rattle and . . ."

"Noquay and Weetop spoke to you?" Winay interrupted, wide-eyed.

Nuda twisted her ankle and barely caught herself with her cane.

"Well!" said Winay. "The turtle men introduced themselves to you, eh birdie? You have been truly blessed."

Nuda emitted something between a sniff and a snort and Winay just brushed her away.

"Not now, Sister. Later."

Their secret subject matter was untouchable. Ashneon

knew better than to question them on topics they did not choose to answer.

Winay broke the tension. "Now, I'll introduce you to the single most important man in the room. He's way up . . ."

"Oh! But . . ." Nuda began, silenced by Winay's golden glare.

"Right up here," Winay resumed firmly. "His name is Hobbo."

"You mean that mean-looking old wooden doll, all dressed in green?" asked Ashneon.

"Shhh! He is far from just an old wooden doll!" replied Winay, winking in an exaggerated manner. "Old Hobbo here was not made by a human being. He was carved by 'the one whose name should not be mentioned.'" Her lips enunciated that last phrase as though she was speaking to a foreigner.

Nuda emphatically echoed the words, "not be mentioned."

"His job is to protect this place," Winay added.

"He looks like a plain old bad spirit to me. What with that green hat and suit, all scraggly faced," Ashneon chastised.

"Beware appearances, birdie! Hobbo can take any form. Observe things more carefully. Remember the lesson of the mask. Anyway, Old Hobbo isn't supposed to be Mr. Nice Guy. He is capable of doing grave harm for the sake of universal balance. He's not *bad,* exactly. Bad is a word you will soon learn to forget. He is just powerful. He is capable of doing bad if necessary. Bad actions for a good purpose, you might say. In simple terms: he maintains the balance."

"Ah, so that's why we've never been robbed?" Ashneon sighed.

"However, there are a few other folks whom its best for you to stay away from altogether. Certain artifacts are only for the men to touch; just like only we women can talk to Pually."

"Here's a fine example." Winay's fumbling wrist gestured toward a stone sealed in a plexiglass box in the nearby case.

"Sister, with Tomuck gone, we'll need Skeezucks to deal with this one."

Nuda grunted.

"It's not particularly lovely," coughed Ashneon.

"It didn't used to be ugly, birdie," said Winay, frowning at Nuda. "It's an otter stone. Only men's energy is compatible with it. One day, many years ago, a foolish young Indian woman picked it up because she thought it was a stunning shade of seaweed green." Winay began to speak like a first grade teacher. "Young people sometimes play with powers they do not fully understand. They do not see the harm their ignorance may bring. The spirit of our friend the otter is now trapped inside this stone until the mark of that woman's touch wears off."

Nuda was carefully examining her black, orthopedic shoes and humming. Winay resumed, trembling a bit and scowling. "She just had to touch it." Her voice cracked. "It'll take another lifetime for its true color to return."

"I'll be sure to leave that one alone," assured Ashneon.

This new information sent the young woman's teeth chattering. "Winay, why did you ever let me spend so much time in those foolish books?" she asked.

"Because I thought that if you had already tried the white man's way when you finally found out the truth, you'd be better able to judge the difference. At least that was my opinion. Tomuck and I disagreed quite a bit on that approach. But I'm a firm believer in the old saying: you can't know sweet 'til you've tasted sour.

"Tashteh's people—can they speak to artifacts, too?"

"Not like us. No. Our ways are our own, Ashneon. That's why we have this museum.

The banks of the Quinnepaug River, between Patuxet and Yantuck territory, suddenly yawned into a wide, unfathomable gulf that none but the bravest transmariner dared cross.

Nuda broke Ashneon's melancholy. "Still, those Patuxets do have their special skills. They sure know how to talk to fire and nobody understands the pipe better than them."

"Nuda, I think we could all use some tea," nudged Winay. "How do you feel about reading cups today? I believe Ashneon has earned a special off-Sunday reading."

The three medicine beings descended the mountain as one. Inside the house, the one wearing the youthful mask swished black tea leaves in a cracked ivory pot while the other two shrank into their seats, worn down from heavy talk.

Ashneon poured her own tea last, then scooted in beside Nuda at the kitchen table.

"Well, well, Ashneon! What have we here?" Nuda revived. "Must be close to the strawberry moon. I see children in your cup!"

"More than one?" Ashneon gasped.

"Oh yes, definitely more than one. They will make you very proud."

Ashneon's face twisted like a crooked mask. Children were the furthest thing from her mind. Nuda just shrugged, pressed her lips together and excused herself.

CHAPTER 15

RISING

Sleeping at the museum had become routine. It was now the center of Ashneon's universe. Wolf spiders scampered in and out of corners, bound by signal threads to the web of life. Having spent so much time with the dead, it was refreshing to be enveloped in life.

The day began with a serious dusting venture into the endless nooks and crannies of the stone room until a sudden mountain tremor knocked her sideways into a whaling trunk. Unwanted guests had arrived. Down below, half a dozen cyporter vehicles vomited modular men with plug-in hair followed by female counterparts sporting their own designer add-ons, all surging up the mountain like a retrovirus.

"I'm headed down," insisted Ashneon as she raced past Winay, who was standing guard with the plant people at the front door.

"Hold your ground, birdie. Hold your ground," Winay instructed.

Aquinnee was hunched beside a cycam, as Skeezucks kicked pebbles. Their eyes were hollow.

"Ms. Quay, How do you feel about your new Oracle?" pressed a cyporter, maintaining his focus on Obed.

"No new Oracles, today. There has been enough upset for Winay Weekum recently. Now is not the time for any more sudden changes here on Yantuck Mountain. If Obed Mockko is meant to become a Medicine Man, what you call an Oracle, it can wait until Winay Weekum is up to formally confirming him."

"You are referring to the elder female Oracle?" the commentator asked.

"No. Winay is our Medicine Woman. But yes, in a manner of speaking, I am, yes," Ashneon fumbled.

Meanwhile, Obed was enrapturing everyone with a pseudo-salutation to the sun. Although it was nothing like the classic version of this yoga exercise where the upper half of the body arches skyward from a prostrate position on the floor. No, Obed's girth prompted an awkward, kneeling improvisation. Nonetheless, the bamboozled media did not take a single commercial break during the entire ludicrous display.

After several focused breaths, the would-be yogi addressed Ashneon's plea for patience. "We should all respect Ashneon's wishes and let this change proceed at the Creator's pace. Praise be to Grandfather Turtle. He is slow, but steady and sure."

Skeezucks clutched the eagle talon at his neck. Ashneon began to reach for his hand then noticed Obed grinning down at her. Tingles ran down her spine as she brushed him aside and trotted up the mountainside and back into the house. There, Winay was pacing and chanting obscenities in Yantuck as though they were prayers.

"Win, everything seems all right for now. What are they still doing down there? Why won't they just go away?"

No reply. The old woman was stroking a leaf of rattlesnake plantain withering in the window.

"Oh Win, where do you go when you disappear like this?" Ashneon sighed.

The young woman plopped into Tomuck's old cychair to complete the torture. The cyscreen was featuring her house, her mountain, her cousin Obed and the poorly replicated sensations of her entire world.

The audio blared, "a grief-stricken and delusionary young woman—yes, those are the words Oracle candidate Obed Mockko just used to describe his cousin, Ashneon Quay. Sources inside New Light Corporation claim Quay to be the only real opponent to Mockko's immediate assumption of the Yantuck Oracle seat and automatic addition to the New Light CorporateWeb Site."

Onscreen, Obed was fondling a chinese silk drawstring bag filled with jade, peridot, malachite, aventurine, and chrysoprase in front of a baby-faced cyporter who smelled like ylang ylang. Just as he commanded the girl-woman to select a Guidance Stone, a more seasoned female cyporter muscled in for an updated commentary on the Ashneon Problem.

"My cousin claims she is acting to protect Oracle Winay Weekum, and we all appreciate her pain, but she must acknowledge that the only one she is protecting is herself. Dear little Ashneon must confront her loss and move on. Denial is a condition that this unfortunate young woman knows only too well. That's quite understandable, really. Unfortunately, the world cannot wait for either her salvation or its own. We Oracles have to weigh the needs of the many against those of any one individual. Besides, I can reassure you that Oracle Winay will be fine. She comes from a great medicine line that doesn't unravel over a natural rite of passage like a death in the family.

He went on with gusto, "I have faith in my aunt Winay Weekum. She saw her people through the desperate times of the early twenty-first century and she will move forward. The real question is, will Ashneon let her? It is now up to Ashneon Quay to put aside her personal feelings and do what is right for all the people of Mother Earth."

Prime time was nearly over, so Obed arched his arms over his head. As the wind slapped his cape into the background, he began the mantra that signaled his standard wind-up. "The New Light surrounds us," he roared. "We must not shade our eyes . . ."

Nearly all the bystanders joined in, including the cyporters, "We embrace the sun. We are one with the light, one with the flame. May the flame burn within us, bright for all to see, as it warms and lights our world, may it unite us as one new light."

The cyporter sighed. A perfect segue.

"Thank you so much, Oracle Obed, for those beautiful insights. We turn now to Dr. Foxon Arber, well-known psychiatrist and scholarly aide to Obed Mockko—soon to be the world's latest greatest online Oracle."

"That bastard," Ashneon hissed. "Win! C'mere! Look who's on now! I didn't even see him down there!"

Foxon began, "Ashneon Quay has enjoyed a lifetime basking in the light of a brilliant Oracle. I refer in this case of course to Tomuck Weekum. When his light was removed, she suffered a condition recently identified in our profession as . . ." Foxon signaled the cameras to zoom in for a close-up, then lowered his voice to a bare whisper, "White Light Deprivation or WLD." He resumed at normal volume, "this condition is akin to withdrawal from narcotics, and it results from the sudden loss of a great spiritual leader. I assure you, it is treatable. I actually came here, originally, to see if I could help the young woman through her time of loss. But as you can see, such treatment takes time and patience, especially when it comes to close followers—those who are the most strongly affected. They crave the enlightenment they are accustomed to receiving from their spiritual leader and react to the denial of that light in negative ways, hence the term White Light Deprivation."

Foxon struck a vogue pose for one luxurious moment before continuing—hand covering his heart, shadow falling across half his face. "This condition is not to be taken lightly. It is far more serious than seasonal physical light deprivation disorders. It not only causes depression and divests an individual of all ability to function normally, it also manifests itself in the form of grave delusions. The best thing for Ashneon, along with her entire Tribe and the rest of the world, is for Obed Mockko to assume his new position as soon as possible. That will fill the gap in their lives and mitigate the effects of WLD. An Oracle to replace an Oracle, a system as old as time. Meanwhile, we ask that everyone pray for the recovery of Ashneon Quay and the Yantuck people during their time of loss."

A filthy halo circled Foxon's head. He had cached himself inside one of those vehicles and waited for just the right moment to pounce. What a weasel. WLD! They were eating it up, devouring bowlful after bowlful of his lies.

The cycam moved in tight as he blew on the end of a glowing stick of copal.

"Would you care to join us in a smudge?" Foxon asked the wide-eyed cyporter.

"Me? Why of course, Dr. Arber!"she licked her lips.

Phermones gushed through the screen. Foxon was a spiritual gigolo who did not even have the decency to shut the bedroom door behind him.

The commentator continued, breathless and giddy. "And on a separate note, Dr. Arber, you have a new cybook coming out, which is of quite some interest?"

"Yes," he lightly stroked the tip of one of her fingers as he spoke. "I have to thank Oracle Obed for his insights which complimented my recent research into the power of ancient objects."

"Uh, um, Dr. Arber, I understand you have, um, been researching scholarly texts for literally decades on this subject. Your previous titles include *Mayan Sky* and *Lakota Sun*. Ladies and gentlemen, this one looks like another winner." She began to fan herself with her notes, "Whew, uh, you can p-purchase Dr. Arber's *Objects of Light* on cybook or cyscript. And you have a special sale, uh, sale or rather, introductory price today, for the, um, next hour, is that right?"

The cyporter was actually panting now. All that was left were
the inevitable moans and groans. Their passion was contagious

and Ashneon dashed up the mountain, hoping to break a sweat before showering. Even Skeezucks could not have scaled the mountain any faster. The flushed cycrew had already packed their equipment.

For Ashneon, this was a moment when it was necessary to secure a victory against some enemy, any enemy. Up at the museum, the books scowled at her, but she ignored them and grinned at the lean wooden soldier who would not let them out of his sight.

"Hobbo, I think this trash belongs down at the house. Let's give our honored guests some breathing room," She scooped an armful of books into a box.

The cardboard buckled en route, allowing only a safe split second for the box to be tossed onto the kitchen counter before immediate self-destruction. Several books flopped over the edge onto the floor and Ashneon kicked them. They were fallen enemies.

"Winay," she called upstairs. "I've got to get out of here. I think I'm supposed to be meeting Tashteh for lunch at Fiddleheads. Looks like the wackos are wrapping it up at the foot of the mountain. I've just got to get out of here for awhile."

"Go on, birdie. Been attacked by plenty worse than that bunch."

About five tissues and three miles down the road, an empty quiet set in. Ashneon called Tashteh on the cy.

"Hey, you, it's only me, the famous Ms. WLD."

"Huh?"

"Weren't we supposed to meet for lunch? That is if you're not afraid I might be contagious."

"I'm sorry, Ashneon, did I forget we were meeting? What is WLD? Are you sick?"

A woman in the background scolded him, "Tashteh, you don't have time for this. We've got to go-ooo."

"Oh, I'm sorry, Tashteh. I must have put down the wrong date. Forget it. I guess you weren't watching the cy. Just a stupid joke," mumbled Ashneon.

The woman in the background continued to mumble. "Tashteh, please."

"Ash? Is everything okay?"

"Everything is just as it should be, Tashteh."

Shamaquin appeared, pointing in the direction of the Weekum House.

"I've got to go too. Bye." Ashneon gulped and hung up. Her mother was not in the habit of making such bold appearances, unless . . .

The plants in the Weekum House entryway were suffocated by cyporters. The door jerked open and Ashneon's knees nearly buckled when she saw Obed's hand resting on top of Winay's.

"Oh, hello birdie," grinned Winay. "Your cousin was just telling me how he is going to help us out, now that Tomuck has moved on. He's willing to do all our speaking to the media on the issues. He says he can keep them all away. And here we were, so worried about who would take over after Tomuck. Seems we're all set now. With Obed on board, you're freed up to do as you please. Don't really need two Medicine Yantuck People, what with all the help Obed'll have around him."

Ashneon stared blankly. She had never considered making her own way in the world. Responsiblility. Obligation. Tradition. That was all she had ever known. That was all any traditional Indian knew. The sudden option of choosing her destiny dizzied and sickened her.

"Winay, why?" Ashneon blinked away tears and rubbed her itchy nose. The stuffy room was infused with vanilla and a host of other edible scents. Ashneon silently vowed never to bake again.

"You'll see, birdie. It will all be fine now," the old woman replied.

"My job is to take away all your worries," Obed cooed at the old woman, massaging his temples.

"Well, congratulations, Oracle Obed," Ashneon stated flatly.

"Medicine Man, Ashneon. He's a Medicine Man now," corrected Winay. "You know how Tomuck felt about that Oracle business."

"I guess you'll be attending the tribal meeting Sunday afternoon?" Ashneon probed. "We have some serious issues before our community." Her eyes burned through the cloud of reporters. "Issues which you and I should discuss privately," she added.

He smiled, "No, Ashneon, that won't be possible. I am sorry. I will not be at the meeting. Tribal meetings are closed to outsiders. As an Oracle—I am sorry Win—as a Medicine Man—I believe that I represent many people now and that I belong to all people. When the tribe opens up its meetings to the world, I will return to them. Until that time, tribal members can address their concerns with me here at my home. We Yantuck need to move beyond our petty nationalist divisions and realize we are all members of the human race, part of the universal union of light!"

"I see, Oracle Obed. So you are home for good this time?" asked Ashneon. "You will be caring for the children at Nuda's?" she maintained the pressure.

"All of Mother Earth is my home. I must go wherever and whenever I am called. The children are in great hands with Nuda, no matter where I am called."

"Blessed be," whimpered West Wind, licking a salty tear off her polished copper lip.

CHAPTER 16
NOISE

Evil gangs of forty-niners had taken up daily residence inside Obed's head. Hey ya. Hey ya. Hey ya ho. There was no rest in sleep, either; for his nightmares featured a mountaintop prison where the bars were made of trees.

Maybe there was a simple explanation for the pounding headaches: like they were caused by the incessant calls from the press or suddenly coping with raising twin children. Or maybe, just maybe, the blame lay with one turquoise-eyed prima donna who was simply driving him nuts. Run-ins with Ashneon definitely made the symptoms far worse. But whatever it was, Obed Mockko's world was exploding with sound. He could scarcely hear his own voice. The only option was to consult with West Wind Monroe for a cure.

Loose gravel rumbled beneath his car as it streaked past rows upon rainbow rows of solar huts, each well ordered and neatly boxed into one eighth of an acre of lawn pavement. The only parking area abutted an odd, leaf-scattered dirt pile, extruding field stones and an oversized tree. The racket in his head raged as he knocked on the key lime door.

"Why, Oracle Obed, you honor me." West bowed, but did not face him directly, which was just as well, since she was sans pigments, lacquers and flowing garb. In fact, she was a hideous mess, much like her house, which smelled like a mad brew of holiday baking and sour laundry.

"I was just consulting with Dr. Foxen about a small difficulty in my practice lately," she demurred.

He ignored the sloppy witch and stepped inside. She had been hard at work, all right. All the New Light staples were heaped into a ritual mound beside her bed. Dragon goblets, effigy rocks, conjuring candles, black cauldrons, crystal wands, and cheap (but elegant) boxes of spiced Indian incense, nothing at all useful for battling big, bad medicine.

The solar hut was not divided into rooms. Bedroom, kitchen, den, and dining areas had all melted into something known as a Sun Space, intended to minimize windows due to electricity rationing. Unfortunately, that meant that piles of crusted dishes and soiled underwear regularly impacted the Wiccan shrine.

Foxon staggered over to the door, straining to widen his swollen eyes, and knotting his oily hair back into a greasy cinnamon bun. Behind him, the cy was scrolling lists of Wiccan remedies, interrupted at regular intervals by an irritating viral blip.

Obed's pupils darted back and forth across the room, as if speed-reading an invisible book. "You two went beyond your limits, didn't you? You did something very wrong. Simple white light Wiccan prayers didn't set me up for this Oracle position. Whatever you used, I know it's connected with these deafening noises in my head, and you have to undo it! NOW!"

"You're right! Okay! You're right! I went against my own coven's best counsel. The noise is all my fault. We tried to make you the center of international commotion and it worked! It worked too well! Oh hell, Foxon tell him!" wailed West, diving for a half-full bottle of Jameson whiskey.

A bedraggled Foxon spilled the rest. "West used a control spell to make you the focus of all things, to center the world's uproar and tumult on you and, more importantly, away from your cousin Ashneon. You're right. She didn't use white light Wiccan magic. But the spell wasn't exactly black magic, either. It was more like gray. So we didn't see the harm. Either way, here we are in the inevitable backlash."

"Find a way to make it stop," directed Obed. "Fast!"

"I'll be honest with you, Obed. We've been trying. But we can't find anything to counteract the noise," he admitted.

Obed gouged the pulsating veins at the back of his neck, then dashed outside to retrieve a red cedar branch from the back of his vehicle. He threw it atop West's spell books and soaked the pile with the contents of his butane lighter, then torched the whole thing. As he strolled into the fire, Foxon yanked him out and signaled for help.

Nuda smelled trouble in the wind.

"I haven't heard from your father today. Did he say when he would be coming home?" she asked Aquinnee.

"Nope. Stopped in for a quick minute a couple hours ago," the girl replied. "Mumbled something about feeling like his head was exploding. Not good. Definitely not good."

Nuda performed the necessary secondary reconnaissance by contacting West, then issued her report to Ashneon via the cy, "Obed's run off. That witch of the west and her golden boy are real fine friends all right. They called the men in white on my son! Hopefully, the fool will be here before too long and avoid their trap. Bring whatever tools you can think of, Ashneon. You'll need them all. Wait, never mind, he's here. I see his car. Looks like he's going past me and straight up to your place! Get ready. Be careful!"

"Absolutely," Ashneon glowed.

Her traditional regalia slid on like a second skin. Ashneon's beaded blouse was covered with carefully selected symbols: the mountain, the turtle, and the tree of life. She also brought the eyestone, just in case.

"Let me in," croaked a raspy voice at the door. "I need your help. You're the only one I respect enough to ask for it."

"Uh huh," grunted Ashneon as she opened the door.

"Thank you," he heaved.

Ashneon instinctively turned away from him. The white gunk in the corners of his mouth gave him a rabid quality. Worse still, his skin appeared glossy and gluey, like he had just hatched from an egg.

"Thank you for taking me in, Ashneon. Did you know that the Gathering of Nations is hosting a drumming competition in my head right now? You know what that's like? Of course not. I hope you never do."

He lowered his voice. "I have been wanting to give you a gift, one that suits the work you do with the dead."

A ratty owl feather emerged from his stained tobacco bag. The mere sight of that Feather of Death should have terrified her but Ashneon carefully examined and considered his gift.

"This owl feather is a one-way ticket, you know," said Ashneon. "You should have kept it for yourself. Then your whole tortured widower drama would be over. You'd be back with your beloved Danugun and the rest of the world would be free from your misery."

Obed laughed. It sounded like a cackle. "I wish I could have gotten off so easy. You know where we're both headed, don't you?" His cape rattled against the screen door. As Ashneon followed him toward the museum, a fierce wind sliced her cheeks and her moccasined toes curled under from the icy hurt.

"Hey, you have no business up there!" she raced behind him.

His cowboy boots scuffed the museum threshold, as he swirled around to face her.

"What is it that you know and I do not?" he asked. "You must have some secret spell, or some special amulet, perhaps?"

Ashneon winced at the thought of the eyestone in her pocket.

"What protects you and throws all my projects back onto

me?" pleaded Obed, clutching his head. He reached for the door handle.

"So you admit it!" she shouted. "Projects got you into this. They triggered that earthquake in your head. How dare you dabble in projects? You know what we were taught. That renegade witch of yours, she started this!"

He turned again, "Ashneon, you must know by now that not everything we were taught was good for us. Yes, I have tried new things. I have questioned. I have *lived*, Ashneon, not just followed the Yantuck lesson plan for life, like you. I wanted more than just this tiny little mountain and its small-minded Indians."

"Well you got more and look at you, you're a mess and you still wound up back here anyway. That says it all. I was always satisfied with this mountain. If you saw it fully, you wouldn't find it so limiting."

Through the window, Hobbo glared down at Obed, eyes fixed like lasers. When Obed glared back, the old wooden doll wobbled toward the edge of the shelf.

"This mountain may limit you more than you know, my dear cousin! Ashneon, I am the Medicine Chief of the mountain now. I may be suffering but at least I am no longer your insignificant cousin. I am no longer just the man who couldn't protect those he loved, not my wife, not my parents, not even you! Now, I am able to meet any challenge. I can climb the highest mountain. Not just here, but anywhere. I am not just some insignificant gnat caught in Grandmother Spider's web. Now, I *am* the web."

His voice began to spin, "You didn't even know I could climb mountains did you? Run from bottom to top? I've done it. I always could. I can fly, too. I bet you've never flown, Ashneon. Never even considered it. You watch the birds every day, probably dreamt about flying but never once tried it. It's not in the Yantuck Medicine Woman's Manual is it? Your legs are chained to this mountain. You do what you are told and accept the destiny you were given. You have only one way out and it's not of this world. Want to watch me fly, Ashneon? 'Cuz you never can. There are a lot of things you can only experience through me. I live life. I can fly. I'll fly down this mountain and far away from here. You have never even tried to fly. Have you, Ashneon? Watch now. 'Cuz you can't do it—ever. So watch me. Watch me fly!"

Obed soared down the path, his colossal arms and legs flailing as he tumbled headlong over the sharp granite steps into the highway. The rocks shredded his cloak and scraped his face. In the middle of the road, he flopped onto his back and flailed his bruised limbs like a vanquished turtle. Ashneon was too stunned to move as the white van pulled up alongside him.

CHAPTER 17
PROJECTS

"Tashteh, I don't know how deep he is into projects. But we should have time to investigate before he gets out. Of course, those shrinks will be useless for what's wrong with him. Their white noise therapy won't do anything to stop that unearthly racket in his head."

"C'mon. Let's go see the henchmen." Tashteh straddled a broom and twisted his face like a hag.

"I can't believe we're back here again in crayola land," said Tashteh. "At least that great tree is still standing."

"Well, Tashteh, somehow I don't think the location of this tree, West's house, and this whole Obed mess is all just a coincidence."

The witch's tiny mailbox was erupting with white and manila envelope corners.

"West?" Ashneon spoke through the flimsy lime door. "We know what has happened. We're here to help you."

West looked like Raggedy Ann, all pale and floppy, tossing spell book after spell book up into the air.

"All right. Let's start by finishing what was already begun," said Ashneon, fingering the eyestone. She threw several books into the remains of Obed's fire pit.

"No, no, no. Not the books," protested West. "That's what Obed was doing when he went crazy."

"Maybe not so crazy," muttered Tashteh.

"No, you can't," insisted West. "I'll never find a cure without these books! So many are damaged already, please, no! My coven does not even allow these spells to go on the cy, because IFORI (International Freedom of Religious Information) would steal them."

Ashneon took West's hands lightly into her own. "Your coven does not allow a lot of things that you went ahead and did anyway. Perhaps now you can atone for your indiscretions by bringing your colleagues back a better truth. Teach them this: there is no real medicine in books or on the cy. Medicine comes from the earth and sky alone. Mother Earth is the first and only true teacher, the source of real knowledge. Ask Mother Earth directly for your answers and you will find them. She is our key to the rest of the universe. Begin with that before tackling the cosmos. Tell your coven that is what you have learned from your mistakes. You are not the first witch to become misguided. You simply forgot the earth-roots of your own medicine."

"The consequences of this ceremony, either way, are grave," pleaded West. Tashteh gripped Ashneon's arm so hard that she winced.

West continued, "the only way to undo a control spell is for one of the people affected by it to take all of its negative energy upon himself. Even then, there may be serious side effects."

"Well, since I am the one this spell drew attention away from, it has to be me. Don't worry. I've come well protected," Ashneon assured them both.

The great Pawtucket Medicine Man was suddenly reduced to a helpless sidekick. Ashneon pointed to the turtle, mountains, and tree on her regalia, then winked, holding up the eyestone. Then, she turned her back on him and took a deep breath. West cast down her eyes and handed Ashneon the stubby gray candle that had begun the whole mess.

"Please be careful," West pleaded. But Ashneon just shrugged, "This is why I am here."

Tashteh's rigid purple jaw told Ashneon that it was now or

never. He fiercely crumpled a few pieces of paper kindling atop the books and ignited the blaze, then lit his pipe from a burning page and forced himself to settle back and commune with the gold and amber flames.

"West," Ashneon summoned. "Pour some of that whiskey of yours into a cup and leave it by the western door. You're not the only one who likes it. Now go!"

Ashneon set the glowing nub of the gray candle down in front of her. The thought of examining it through the eyestone made her shiver. But there was no turning back. It was time to beckon the forces of change.

"Spirits of the four winds, protectors of the plants, animals, and beings of Yantuck Mountain, we ask that all that has been brought by the medicine of this foreign candle be removed. Return the spell to the land it came from, harming no one of that place. Any poisons remaining from its visit here, let them remain here and enter me, and only me, never again harming anyone or anything of this or any place."

The air instantly reeked like Saturday morning at the Boulderton fish docks. West keeled over and puked a colorful spray without making a sound. The room dimmed and a hot gust of air burned their eyes shut.

CHAPTER 18

INDIAN GIVER

One Week Later

The Mockko House was silent. Every day, Ashneon inspected its exterior for signs of life and found none. She wondered if Obed had embarked upon another global quest and decided to cart Nuda and the twins along with him this time.

After two full weeks had passed she could wait no longer and plowed into Nuda's kitchen. Nope, Obed was still there, sitting right next to half a dozen or so bags of rotting garbage. He did not even notice her. His mind was lost in the same old forest, where he was bound and determined never to be found. He believed that the condition of being lost made him important. After all, a child lost in the woods commands national attention. A lost teenage girl terrifies police with suspicions of rape and murder. Even a lost dog drives a community to distraction with postings on every corner. Unfortunately, Obed forgot that a lost man is always suspect and a lost Indian man does not even stand a chance. He is either in trouble with the Law, late on his child support, out on a bender, or running around on his woman. No one loves a lost Indian man, least of all himself.

Still, he was no longer wearing black and upon close examination, there was not a single hint of his former self. Something stronger than witchcraft had turned him into just another beer-bellied skin with a thinning ponytail in beat-up jeans and a forest green pow wow t-shirt.

She interrupted his hopeless wanderings. "How did you avoid the cyporters? Where are they all?"

"Oh, that's right. You're living the hermit life these days, following in your late great uncle's reclusive 'never leave the mountain' footsteps. Not keeping up with the cy either, are you? Well, I'll catch you up: those New Light folks won't be coming around here anymore. I'm yesterday's news. There's some new Indian medicine marvel up in British Columbia. Seems my little bout with bad medicine made me bad copy. The New Light corporate counsel has disavowed any official connection with me. They said I had never been 'formally approved' as an Oracle. My file has been deleted, which, as you know, means that I am forever blackballed from the cy. As for Foxon and West, they have long since skipped town.

His voice began to squeak slightly. "Funny how neither of them came down with WLD after my fall from grace. Coincidentally, they are in Canada too, following the white light, no doubt. I engineered a scam—according to their official story. So, I'm back to being just Obed Mockko, no more Master Obed, no Oracle Obed, not even Medicine Man Obed. I had to turn that one back, too—to save Winay from being dragged into this mess. Now I am simply Obed of Nothing and Nowhere. So if you don't mind, I just want to sleep now, until it's my time to be with Danugun for good!"

He dropped his head onto the table with a thunk.

"Aw dee baw ba!" scoffed Nuda, appearing out of nowhere. "No sense sleeping your life away. You'll be getting a whole lotta sleep before you know it. Everybody does. Time goes by. Sleep is the one thing everybody gets enough of eventually."

"Oh, I've got it!" Ashneon poked her nose right into his cheek. "How about a new title like The Self Pity Prince! Even though Danugun doesn't think of you that way."

"Oh, man! Now of all times, you have to mention her and kick me when I'm down," he whimpered.

"I hate to interrupt your wallowing, cousin. But may I ask if your head noises are gone?" asked Ashneon.

Obed's shoulders softened and he raised his head, but still refused to make eye contact.

"That's better," she said. "Now be thankful. Be thankful for *something,* anyway. Giving thanks is the most important task we have upon this earth. When we give thanks, we remind the Creator that some of us still love Mother Earth and all of cosmic creation. Love it from right here where we stand. For now, just focus on the simple things, like giving thanks. Keep remembering to give thanks and you'll feel a whole lot better. Be out basking in the sunlight in no time."

"Why bother?" he groaned.

"My dear cousin, the fact that a few human beings continue to give thanks is why the Creator has seen fit not to launch Armageddon already! Be thankful for the mountain that gave you life and brought forth your extraordinary children! Be thankful for what you had with Danugun that some will never have!"

Obed struck a deer-in-the-headlights pose.

Ashneon changed her tone. "I do not mention Danugun to harm you. You always forget how much she meant to me, too. I just want to let you know she still cares about all of us and that you can talk to her. Maybe now you'll want to, because you've acknowledged that she has gone to the other side."

"Cousin, you don't know the half of it with me and Danugun. We shared something ancient. Why would you want to help me anyway, after everything that's happened? What is your gain in all of this?"

"Helping ease pain is what medicine people do! Whether it's the pain of humans, plants, or other entities doesn't matter. It's what I was trained for. It is my responsibility. If I know how to help you, it is my duty to do so. Seeing the future, casting spells, contacting the dead, those are just minor magics performed toward the main function. Ask Winay why she chose me. I'm just following her instructions—something I know you don't understand just yet—and to perform the level of medicine I speak of means upholding traditions and obligations, not simply jumping at opportunities. In spite of what Wall Street thinks."

A yellowed newspaper clipping fluttered in his guarded hand. She eased up again. "I have never hated you, Obed. In you I saw someone who had a clear and shining path right close by, but instead chose a dim, distant path filled with briars. The Beautiful Path leads well beyond this world. You know that. But for us, for who and what we are, it has to start right here on this mountain. Remember when you were able to show Danugun the hiding place of every amber mushroom on the mountain?"

That did it. Obed had disintegrated into mush. That was one step farther than she had hoped. Ashneon was shooting for a more flexible, pliable Obed. Not a destroyed one.

"Danugun was perfect for me." He shoved his late wife's crumbling newspaper photograph into her face. "She meant more to me than medicine. She was medicine, old medicine. That's how I knew, deep down, I wasn't chosen for that path. Danugun had something I would always lack. You don't really want a medicine position, either. Don't lose your chance to have what Danugun and I lost. Don't let that happen to you. Marry Tashteh and choose happiness."

"Whoa! Tashteh and I share our medicine woes, nothing at that level." It suddenly hurt Ashneon to breathe, to exist.

Obed pressed on. "Tashteh loves you as much as a man can. I see what you do not. You may know medicine, but sometimes you miss the boat on life, cousin. The simple, womanly stuff has always slipped by you, like the fact that Wunneah Tatoon is telling everyone that she is going to marry Tashteh Sook. And if you sit still and do nothing about it, then, well . . ."

Ashneon slumped against the kitchen counter like she had been shot in the chest. The color drained from her face and her legs deserted her.

Responsibility. Obligation. Tradition.

Or Love?

"Obed, maybe neither of us is meant for happiness at this level."

"Knowing you, Ashneon, if you don't marry him, you can guarantee your unhappiness."

"My dear cousin, I'm afraid Tashteh only sees me as a good friend and if, by some odd chance, I ever did marry Tashteh, I would be guaranteeing his unhappiness. Husband, home, and the Patuxet Tribe are not my priorities. Anyway, right now we need to speak to Danugun, not so much for you as for her. C'mon. Let's go down to the Cedar Swamp Burial Ground and see if you can visit Danugun with me this time."

"I really hate going to that burial ground."

"That is what we are trying to change. Remember, you must trust me or you will surely fail."

The bizarre image of Danugun standing in front of her own headstone was still emblazoned on Obed's broken heart. As soon as he saw the headstone again, his eyes glazed over. When a figure darted past, he could not make it out, for it moved like the wind.

"Give me your right hand. Put your left hand on the head-stone. Now close your eyes and think of the mountain. Remember you are a part of this Mountain, you have never really left it, ever. And you will never leave it when you die, either. All the beings that ever lived here live here still, just as surely as the chosen live among the stars. Danugun is still here with us. We just need to journey to the space she occupies. Now focus. Here we go.

Ashneon lifted onto her toes and heaved her chest, as though preparing to jump off a high diving board. "The earth has veins, filled with life-giving water. Our bodies have veins, filled with blood. Feel the blood rushing through your veins. Feel its journey in and out of your heart. Now connect with the Mountain and feel the water in her veins. Feel it rushing, rushing, moving you along its stream. Get ready to jump into that stream, get ready to travel deep inside the earth, to meet Danugun. Now, Obed! Jump!"

Ashneon felt as though she had been tossed out of the other side almost as soon as she entered. That had never happened before. A warm zephyr blew the hair across her face as she zoomed back into the living world.

Obed was gripping his face with his hands.

"Relax, cousin," she told him. "It will work next time."

"What? You don't even know, do you Ashneon? She came back again! My Danugun was right next to me, crossed over again, as though you and she traded places. Only she said this was the last time that would be possible! She said we could still talk to each other—only not this way. Something about me needing to climb Nuda's back stairs to see her from now on. Made no sense to me, but she said Nuda would know. She insisted that I move on for Aquinnee and Skeezucks's sake. Something about their heavy task. Thank you, cousin."

"Huh? Obed, I wish I could take the credit, but I did not bring Danugun over. Not the last time and definitely not now. I don't have that kind of power alone," insisted Ashneon. "It takes at least three to muster that sort of magic."

He extended his open palm. "Perhaps," he acknowledged. "the spirits of Yantuck Mountain have seen fit to give me a second chance. Let me see that gray owl feather I gave you. I need to take back some things."

"On one condition: that you and I issue a joint press release, stating that come this year's pow wow, two new Yantuck Oracles will be ready to assume their responsibilities."

CHAPTER 19
FIREFLIES

The answering machine was full. At sundown, Tashteh gave up trying to call and headed for Yantuck Mountain.

Meanwhile, Ashneon beat her head into the sympathetic down pillow. Obed should have minded his own business instead of dredging up embers from smouldering ashes. Now, she could not smother the inferno within.

"Ashneon, can we go for a walk?" Tashteh yelled upstairs.

"Sure!" She flopped out of bed and splashed water onto her swollen face. "You really didn't need to come by. I'm fine. I'm all set about Obed and West and Danugun. That's all past us now. I just needed some rest. Could be the heat."

"It's not the heat and I know you're all set with them. We need to talk about us. C'mon." She tumbled down the last stair as he hauled her outdoors.

"W-what do you mean? We're fine, Tashteh. We'll always be fine. Your destiny lies across the river."

She continued to ramble on beneath the glowing copper sunset. "I'm so grateful that you were right there for me when Tomuck died. But Winay and I are okay, now. You can't spend your whole life supporting me through disaster after disaster. Your medicine position is the priority now and soon you'll have other commitments . . ."

"Stop. No other commitment is more important than you. Am I that bad at showing how I feel?" he asked.

His hands slipped over hers like soft mittens.

"I think everyone in the world knows that I love you, except you, and that includes Wunneah Tatoon. Oh, don't think I haven't heard the rumors. Frankly, I don't care what any other woman wants. And I know what I want. I want *you*."

The moist earth soaked her moccasined toes as she stretched to meet his lips.

"Ashneon, I can't even imagine life without you." Tashteh wrapped around her like a thick saddle blanket, so safe and so familiar. "You mean everything to me. I'm sick every day I can't see you."

She choked on a sob. "I'm sorry. I thought . . . I guess I've been confused."

The sore, aching spot right between her shoulder blades had vanished.

"I'm so sorry," she repeated.

"Don't you be sorry. Wunneah Tatoon can go straight to hell." He squeezed her hands and smiled.

"You know, I've been thinking pretty much that same thing lately!"

They both giggled.

"So, Ashneon Quay, will you marry me and end all these stupid rumors?"

She froze, as if heartsore for a millisecond, then nodded. Their mouths brushed in feathery kisses, the sort that bring soft smiles on lonely nights for years to come. They could not let go. Tashteh was quite sure that he had not known happiness until that very moment. Ashneon drew a deep breath and threw back her head to survey the vast blackness of the universe.

How silly for so much space to carry so little light!

Spring mattered for the very first time and Tashteh was her world. Indulging in earthly love required spending more time with the living than the dead. So once again, the artifacts had

only the old folks to keep them company.

The Medicine couple had it all: a strawberry moon, a bit of woods, watchful ancestors, ancient traditions, and each other. Their world was nearly whole, and such wholeness was unsettling. Living in pieces was standard. The modern Indian world was a fractured jigsaw puzzle. A few key pieces had been lost for good, so the puzzle would never be complete again, and like all misfit goods, it would eventually be thrown away. But on this, the eve of the summer solstice, the lingering sun shone for them alone.

They deserted their regular haunts of burial grounds, rock sites, and Indian reservations to approach the Garden City rose garden at dusk. Ashneon had traded in her dreary velvets for a cotton candy look. Confectionary colors had begun to appeal to her.

Tashteh had also loosened up a bit. But only a bit. One thick, tightly woven braid fell down his broad back. Ashneon had nearly the same hairstyle save one thin, additional braid, woven with scarlet hemp that trickled down her left side. They joked about that. Simplicity did not suit her.

The rose garden was the last remaining plantscape in Garden City. The city's downtown was an abandoned fire trap wedged between Boulderton and the rez. A *filius nullius* / land without heritage—a place no one called home. A cyberfest blasted sensations from the big paved area in the center of town, once called the Green. There was nothing green about it now. The quest for parking had paved the world. At least the city's name had protected this solitary patch of flora from the pioneering pavement. Few people even remembered the rose garden anymore. It was not cared for like the old days when prize-winning roses were the highlight of an annual fair. Now, those once-elite rose bushes tangled with lowly bull briars and mangy field grass.

The summer sun reveled in its last moment of glory, til the

creatures of the night could wait no longer. Ashneon caught her breath and swallowed hard. The annual gathering of wa-wa-tay-see was underway. Those fireflies were her favorite creatures. An entire race of beings who cast their collective light to brighten the night. For all the strawberry moons spinning back to the beginning of time, they had chosen this time of year to mate. When their light was most brilliant, they joined for a brief, gleaming moment of joy. They had survived because they were adaptive creatures, whose native rituals now included even the foreign-born roses. On this night, they twirled and blinked through the balmy perfumed air like waltzing stars.

"I live to lie down on moss," said Ashneon, smoothing a fuzzy patch beside a flaming rose bush.

A scarred wrought iron sign read *Ambra Rosata*. Tashteh lay beside her, surveying the tiny creatures of light, performing their dance of love and life. The couple rolled over in a gentle wave. With a mattress of moss, a headboard of roses, and a blanket of fireflies, they lay in a bed that was truly alive. No tribal ceremonies to organize, no ancient practices to defend against New Lighters. The festival rumbled in the background, but the fireflies drowned it out, with the aide of chirping crickets and gently swishing breezes.

Tashteh shared many dreams with Ashneon that night. Dreams of children, dreams of a better future for their people—starry-eyed dreams.

With Tashteh's Medicine title now official and Ashneon dubbed Tomuck and Winay's heir apparent, there were, of course, some probing questions that remained: Where to live? How to balance all the duties and responsibilities?

But for now, none of that mattered. Tashteh Sook and Ashneon Quay chose to behave like natural creatures for the very first time. As Tashteh craned his neck to admire the fireflies, Ashneon slipped her arms around his waist. He nibbled the top of her head, and she strained upward, catching only the stubble of his chin.

A constellation of shimmering wings reflected in his dark eyes, as he pressed her into their mossy bed.

Life is fire. Life is light.

For a brief moment, he pulled away and halted, while a hazy glow encircled them both. The moss fell away and they ascended until frozen in flight just above the treetops, blinking down upon the flaming rose bushes.

Now was their moment. Two medicine beings wrapped around one another, moving in synchronicity.

Flickering fireflies.

CHAPTER 20
∪PSETTING THE BALANCE

The mountain no longer swaddled her like a familiar cradle-board. Its protective shields had vaporized and prickly warn-ings popped up everywhere. Each morning, the seed beads, carefully sewn onto the bridal regalia the previous day, were found scattered across Nuda's sewing table. The red and yellow ribbons on Tashteh's calico shirt mysteriously frayed into fluffy, tangled knots. Small snafus with big implications.

Small minds were also a problem. Tribal elders on both sides of the river battled over whose jurisdiction the ceremony would fall under and whether the succotash would be made with or without onions. Neither the Yantucks nor the Patuxets were known to compromise, so not even the tiniest issue was quibble-free.

Things were slowly falling apart as legions of bad spirits mer-rily frolicked about the mountain. Even Winay's spiritual arsenal of ancient ceremonial stones, sweetgrass, wampum necklaces, and eagle feathers could not force them away because they had been invited by the bride and groom themselves—when they chose to break the rules.

It is an age-old fact. Medicine People are not supposed to marry one another. Too much energy concentrated in one place is always dangerous—dangerous to the couple, danger-ous to those around them, dangerous to the universe. So it was no surprise that Yantuck Mountain quaked with spiritual rumblings.

"Mom! I am not a fool! I know my own visions!" screeched

Wunneah Tatoon. "Remember, it was your great-great-grandmother who convinced me that I was to become the next Mrs. Tashteh Sook! Why can't you understand my situation? I am simply following the instructions of those on the other side. Have you forgotten your own teachings on dream-visions? Nothing you can say will stop me. I am bound by my orders. Tashteh will be here any second and I am going with him on that trip!"

Mrs. Tatoon swallowed a sigh, much like the men did around her daughter. Tashteh did not even notice the two squawking beauties in the foyer. Unlike other Patuxet men, he was immune to the charms of the Tatoon women. Too much lightness of being. Only heavy medicine seduced him. An Indian girl who walked and talked with the dead had captivated his earliest childhood admiration.

Wunneah ran three, frosty-pink fingernails down her neck, then probed the beaded barrette crowning her head. Not one silky lock dared stray from that fastidious ebony bundle.

"Hello, Tashteh." She placed an artful fingertip upon his forearm. "I'm going with you to Louisiana. I set up our local Healing Conference here last month, so the Tribal Council wants me to attend your gathering as well. They've already okayed it. Which train will we be taking?"

"No, Wunneah. That won't work. I'm scheduled for tomorrow at the crack of dawn," he excused. "Besides, I have to see Ashneon before I go."

Wunneah turned her back on him, ostensibly examining an old Pow Wow poster on the wall. "I'm taking care of everything for you. I'll handle the cyporters, too." She dabbed her eyes then turned back to say, "you won't need to . . ."

But he was already gone.

"Hello, Tashteh?"

"Ashneon? Are you sure you want me to go? Are you really feeling all right?" Tashteh asked.

For a hollow moment, he heard only the cawing of the mountain crows.

"Of course. Don't mind me. I'm fine. Besides, I haven't seen enough of Aquinnee and Skeezucks and their summer vacation is nearly over. Have a good time and don't rush back. Nothing ever changes around here."

That was a double lie. The twins would be away with Nuda on the Cape for another week and the newly-formed crevices beneath her eyes stemmed directly from a recurring dream. Night after night, she revisited the same irksome scene:

Gold and amber lava bubbled with life onto a barren land, then sizzled into a black sea. Beneath its waves, gleaming creatures bobbed about, visages from an age beyond memory. As the volcanos grew gray and still, the old faces dimmed into nothingness and the sun grew blinding, filtered only by flocks of giant birds and a shower of gold and amber leaves that rained from the brilliant sky.

Sweat-tossed nights were followed by more coffee-driven days. The folks on the other side had not spoken to her in months. Even the artifacts remained mum. All of these factors contributed to a harmful imbalance. Ashneon was not surprised that her stomach was way off again. Nothing went down right.

Tomorrow, Nuda would return soon and conduct an emergency tealeaf reading. In the meantime, Ashneon stared longingly at the teacup rack, where rows of porcelain red roses stood ready to forecast her future.

Obed had refused to accompany the children on their summer pow wow trail, which always culminated with the Yantuck's own annual fiasco. But Ashneon reassured him,

"Indians recall almost nothing of their recent history. You will find that by next year, nobody in Indian Country will even remember Oracle Obed."

It was late Saturday afternoon. Time to lock up the museum until Tuesday. Winay was not doing well again.

"I'm up." Winay patted Ashneon's hand as the girl kissed her forehead.

"Do what you gotta do, birdie," whispered the old woman.

Ashneon shuffled out, then doubled back to hug her grandmother a little too tightly.

"Whoa, birdie. You're gonna break me in two."

Today, the mountain path was longer and steeper. Halfway up, Ashneon leaned against the mangy apple tree, already winded.

How had Tomuck managed to scale that mountain everyday?

A sharp twinge fully doubled her over and she gripped the railing until it passed. Ashneon was generally a firm believer in thinking yourself well. Force the bad spirits away and you'll be fine. Mind over matter. By the time she reached the museum door, she still did not feel fine.

A vine kissed the hollow of her cheek as she entered the museum.

"How is everyone today? Feeling any more talkative? Tomuck? I won't ever leave you, you know."

Halfway between the berry basket and the splintered window sill hung a monstrous web. A decade ago, when Winay used to say, "spiders are good luck," Ashneon would crinkle up her nose and stick out her pointy tongue. But not anymore; now she adored spiders.

A wasp curled into a desperate ball, tugging hopelessly at the huge, sticky orb. With her egg sac full and her days numbered, the pregnant spider stood ready to pounce. The wasp's blood would extend her life for one last all-important day.

Ashneon wished the spider woman well and bid her a safe passage to the other side.

Through the deadly rings, Ashneon viewed the Longhouse.

Nuda must have forgotten to leave out extra suet and songbird seed; the usual twitterings and chirpings were nowhere to be found; only the squawk of a lonely blackbird.

Had the school kids left their garbage inside the Longhouse again?

Better to check now than discover the messy remnants of a rowdy raccoon party in the morning.

As Ashneon edged toward the Longhouse, something flashed by. She touched her cheek and teeter-tottered. It was burning hot. Inside, just behind the buckskin curtain, she spied that blackbird, snacking on paper bag lunch droppings. No other creatures were in sight. She cupped her chin. It was time.

An invisible knife gutted her groin, followed by hundreds of phantom razors slashing and slicing between her legs in synchronicity. There was no way to remain standing, so she stumbled into the stone mortar. As it thumped from side to side on the dirt floor, thick syrupy life gushed from between her thighs, like some hideous potion pouring into mortar. Her feet went frosty, but she dragged her limp legs behind her. A scarlet trail streamed across the lawn as she pulled herself toward the museum threshold. Clumps of chestnut hair stuck to the doormat, caught in the whirlpool of life that circled her head. And all the while, the red-winged blackbird hardly moved.

The phone remained an impossible three feet away and there beside it lay a fallen Hobbo, his missing leg wedged into the far corner of the room. The wooden man smiled tenderly at her, then began to chuckle.

Ashneon flopped onto her back and laughed deliriously.

"Goodbye, Hobbo," she choked as her eyes drifted shut. "Watch after the children for me."

$$\text{✦ ✦ ✦}$$

"We meet again, Ashneon Quay," oozed a familiar voice.

A radiant woman, wearing a turban of fire, knelt beside her. It was Sigi Malinke.

"Follow me," Sigi commanded.

And Ashneon did follow, to a safe, warm, gold and amber place, far beyond pain, way down deep in the fiery womb of Mother Earth, where their hearts beat together as moments, seasons, eons passed.

Another face appeared. It was Tomuck.

"Well done, Ashneon. Your children are fine now, secure in their chosen place. You have given them life and light. You will be better able to help them from here. We will meet again soon. All your questions will be answered by another," Tomuck pointed upward.

It was Shamaquin, hovering overhead, radiant with the luminescence of galaxies, free from all the dim shadows of the living world. To be together again with her mother forever— the fulfillment of her greatest wish.

"Mother." The sudden change in the sound of her own voice startled Ashneon. Her speech was sharp and sure, like tinkling crystal bells.

"Ashneon, I have wanted to tell you so much, birdie. But you needed to draw your own conclusions. From here, we may not pass on all our knowledge to the living, only the way to that knowledge—which takes longer than any single human lifetime. Anyway, all will be revealed in time."

"Have I left the mountain forever?" asked Ashneon.

"No. Your walk among the living is surely done, but you are still needed on the mountain now more than ever. You are for-ever part of Yantuck Mountain. It's just that you are about to see it fully for the very first time. It is time to bid farewell to the mask. Goodbye to the Longhouse, the museum, the Weekum House. Time to blink away the blindness of living and unmask the true wonders of the galaxy. Time to move closer to the truth. There is so much yet to see."

Tomuck rejoined them. "So, Medicine Girl, now you see it: Medicine People are the same everywhere. We all have the universe as well as our own special place, the one born of fire that reconnects us to that burning universe, the place where we meet our bright beginning and our brilliant end. The only real darkness lies in the in-between—and you never were much for the in-between. Welcome home."

CHAPTER 21

MAKING MEDICINE

One Month After Ashneon's Burial

The Tainus were famous for nonconformity. A few tribal members claimed that was because they were not really Indians at all. Of course, no one made that claim in front of Winay Weekum. She defended Ryan, Weeroum, and Anaquah Tianu with the madcap fury of a nor-easter.

The Tainu home nested atop sheer cliffs in a corner of the Yantuck Indian Reservation, shunned by other houses. Opaque faux-mica windows were embedded in its New England granite façade. All transparent glass was confined to the rear of the building, which jutted precariously over the Quinnepaug Gorge—a juxtaposition that made little sense to those who did not remember the days when nosy tourists menaced Yantuck Mountain.

Inside, light splashed through cool rice paper panels onto stucco walls, creating a soothing blend of far east and wild west—except for the hard steel fixtures that iced up every room. Winay defended the family's bizarre sense of style, saying, "the Tianu house has held up better than those flimsy HUD houses, with their mildewed vinyl siding and crumbling, substandard cement."

At the center of the ten-foot cyscreen, Anaquah wrinkled her bushy auburn brow at the image of an amber sunset radiating behind a boastful watch crow. Aquinnee and Skeezucks squinted in the same direction but from their vantage point at the back of the enormous room, they saw only what appeared to be a glowing black-eyed susan.

The words "Winged Messengers" tore across the cyscreen in blinding white laser light, followed by a shot of the earth from space in which the planet sprouted half a dozen verdant, eden-esque patches capped with a joyous flapping crow, each indicating branch locations for "Winged Messengers." Intermittently, the words "Fly With Us" and "Spread the Message" flashed onto the screen while a hypnotic musical score enticed would-be members with a Celtic-Andean melody.

"No, no, no," cursed Anaquah. "This is all wrong. That crow still looks too arrogant against the sunset, too bold, too much like a human being. But the soundtrack is perfect, Aquinnee. Thanks for letting me use your composition. Skeezucks, maybe you could play a traditional flute composition for the new link."

"Sure, Anaquah!" his face reddened and his voice momentarily spiked an octave. "But you're never going to make this work, you know. Turning the cy into an agent of protection for the natural world! Right! Please listen to how stupid that sounds."

Aquinnee fluttered her arms above her head and wailed at her brother, "she's looking for cybersalvation!"

Skeezucks choked on that one, spitting a stream of cranberry juice clear across the faux leather couch.

"You two are as bad as your uncle Tomuck was," said Anaquah. "Tech can be used to save the natural world, not just to ravage it. Tech and spirit are not mutually exclusive. Change is not *always* bad. Cybersalvation may be all that's left!"

The Mockko twins both gulped. It was difficult to stay serious around Anaquah, especially today, with her auburn hair all stuck up and her tee-shirt splattered with impossible mathematical equations like some midget Einstein.

"Where do you come up with these things?" asked
Aquinnee.

"And how old are you, really?" chimed in Skeezucks. "I don't care what kind of genius you may be Anaquah Tianu, you can't convince me that the cy can be used for good."

"Just think about it for a minute, Anaquah," injected Aquinnee. "Delphi I is going up this week. That Spiritual Space Station crap is supposed to join tech with spirit, right? Well, even *you* think that's nuts. Have you seen the medicine morons they picked to go up in that thing? Some of them even have the nerve to call themselves Native Medicine People."

"'Avatars among the stars.'" Skeezucks poked the golden star on Anaquah's shoulder and pumped his eyebrows up and down. "Pa- leeze."

"Okay. Well, you two dyads may be partly right." Anaquah shoved her crooked glasses halfway back up her nose. "My father says I was born under a crazy sun. So fine, laugh if you want to. But this *is* the answer to the paradox that Ashneon struggled with. I'm sure of it. She knew the old ways protected the planet, but she also knew the cy had potential to save it. Besides, she knew there is more to the universe than just your precious Mother Earth. She just never figured out how to mate the old and new before she, well . . ."

Aquinnee grimaced. "Looks like she's got us on that one, Skeezucks. You know Ashneon did everything she did for us. Maybe this is a way for us to do something for her."

Nuda's back stairs remained a majestic memorial to the magical Irishman who blew in on the west wind one fateful day. But those once-lively steps now harbored only empty echoes. After Ashneon passed into the Spirit World, Nuda's grandchildren never again tripped lightly on them, nor anywhere else for that matter. Day after day, the twins plodded around aimlessly while, their father, Obed, remained perched on the middle staircase landing staring longingly into the hollow eyes of Fin Ohgma's carved wren.

There remained only one person who could still add light and levity to the family's gray world.

Anaquah shouted from outside the Mockko house, "who's ready for the watch crow? CAW CAW CAW!"

Their secret signal. Skeezucks and Aquinnee flew outside. Meanwhile, inside Nuda's kitchen two old women shared secrets of their own.

"Obed and the children have been taking this awfully hard," heaved Nuda. "The man is drowning in guilt and he says he worries for the twins."

"It'll pass, Sister," promised Winay. "I guarantee it. Remember, you have a blind spot when it comes to your son. Besides, Aquinnee and Skeezucks have been a bit perkier the last couple days since they've been hanging around with that bubbly Tianu girl."

Nuda dropped her voice down to a raspy whisper, "Win, I gotta ask just one more time: are you sure Ashneon never told you that she was . . ."

"Oh, here we go again," said Winay, wild-eyed and almost shouting. "You do go on. For the hundredth time, no! And I don't think she knew herself. Who ever heard of such a thing in this day and age? I just don't think she had a clue. I really don't. Those things just don't happen anymore."

Nuda's head lolled about pitifully, "and poor Obed had to be the one to find her like that and him being such a klutz and all. Lucky it was only a leg he broke trying to help her, and not his neck. As if he hadn't had enough trauma already this year."

Winay stared at her sister's smooth, radiant skin and wondered how it was that Nuda remained wrinkle-free.

"Nuda, can we please stop reliving poor Obed's trauma. I tell you, he will be fine. Fact is, he's never been better. Fuss over someone else for a change, why don't you? I'm still thinking of my poor granddaughter. Now there's a real tragedy. All ready to take my place, she was, and now I'm still here while she's on the other side. Never did want my medicine position did she? And that poor young man of hers! Blaming himself for going away on tribal business when there was nothing he could have done. Ectopic pregnancy! Never heard of anyone dying from trying to have a baby except my two girls. No there was nothing that boy could have done. Nothing."

"Oh, now, Sister," scolded Nuda. You always told me that all things happen for a reason. Now here I am, reminding you of it. At least it wasn't Bawba's fault this time. My, uh, father has recently assured me that there will be absolutely no more arranged marriages here on Yantuck Mountain."

Winay hrumphed.

Nuda ignored her. "Now things will just go the way they go from now on between the young men and women. The tea leaves say this whole scenario was written by the powers that be. Anyway, young Tashteh Sook'll be all right—have a lovely wife and family soon enough. I seen that in the leaves, too. Don't help us none with our loss, I know. But he'll move on. That Wunneah woman will hold a different appeal for him now.

Nuda's great hand swallowed up Winay's palm, "He was meant for this world, Win, and Ashneon's job was to show him just how much he truly wanted it. Ashneon—well, she was different. She was drawn to the other side. Bawba saw to that right from the beginning. Blazed through life she did, but only for a short while. Just couldn't keep that raging fire burning for long. Seemed like she burnt pine and not oak; that girl had a brilliant flame with no heat or staying power, if you know what I mean."

"But now who will replace Tomuck and me?" Winay was almost whimpering. "What with Ashneon gone and Obed no longer an acceptable choice."

Nuda was not about to allow her sister to slip back down the drain again. So she prodded on. "Sunny side up Win. Sunny side up. Tomorrow's Sunday. That means it will have been a moon since that dreadful funeral. The Pow Wow is in ten days. We need to have answers for the whole world by then. You know that our family's Medicine always opens up the ceremony. Lord knows them fools on the Tribal Council will be asking you about who'll be doing it soon enough.

"Here's my plan," she continued with zest. "Let's all have Sunday dinner together tomorrow. The young people need it and I can give a special reading for you and Aquinnee. It'll do us all good. And maybe you and I can sit together early in the morning and sort things out. I'll make the dinner. Don't you trouble yourself about the meal. I've got one good-sized jar of Ashneon's mushrooms left and this week'll see the last of the good corn and beans for succotash. We can have soup and sandwiches. Don't worry about a thing. I'll do it all.

That last bit clinched the deal. Winay felt it was high time to eat those mushrooms. Besides she hated cooking.

"Beautiful," said Winay. "See you at sunrise. Guess I better go close up the museum. I'm all there is today. I just keep expecting to see Ashneon."

"Oh, you probably will," mumbled Nuda.

The two matriarchs sauntered through the dew, scheming over weak cupfuls of decaffeinated coffee. The crows had already begun squawking and a feisty red-headed woodpecker wacked away at a narrow oak branch. As the wind whistled through the newly drilled hole, it sang an ancient song that made the old women smile. On Yantuck Mountain, dawn was a particularly lively source of pep and inspiration.

Aquinnee and Skeezucks arrived early with Obed, limping along behind them on crutches. But Winay and Nuda were ready. As the twins scurried into the Weekum House, the much-pecked oak tree bowed low, exposing her silvery underskirt. On the topmost branch, a plump crow shouted orders like a drill Sargent.

In the living room, an ecoalert blasted on the cy. "Biggest Icebergs Yet Break Free, Most Dangerous So Far."

Soothsayers and scientists were in agreement for the first time: human beings did not have long to go. Others would replace humanity before too long unless something shifted, and those others would likely be green.

Until humanity's last gulp of breathable air, the people of Yantuck Mountain would continue much as they always had. The thirteen moons would cycle each year. The rocks would continue to mark the sites of ancient miracles, and the blazing sunshine would allow the glorious trees to grow ever thicker; thus, the Yantuck had done their job.

Nuda nudged Obed with her cane. The jar of amber pineo mushrooms, in her steady hands, shone like a precious gem.

"We'll be having the last of these today. Take a look away from that cy and out the window. See that sky. Pretty soon, be time to gather some more for canning. It's time you took Skeezucks mushrooming, you know," she insisted.

Around the world, mushrooming was the stuff of legend. A handful of natural men and women, tucked away here and there, still practiced the old art. Obed's fondest memories included visions of snowy Indian pipe popping up in dainty patches on drizzly mountain mornings, signaling the best mushrooming weather. Those were the days when the adults had instructed him, "take your little cousin Ashneon along and keep her mind off her parents." That was his first real medicine assignment and his first colossal failure. All her life, Ashneon had wished to be with her mother on the other side and Obed could not change that.

Long ago, Nuda had taught Obed that the mushrooms growing in the oak stumps of Yantuck Mountain were magical—so magical in fact that they were even known to grant an extraordinary wish or two. Once little Ashneon obtained that information, she was more eager to tag along with her big cousin. But over the course of the last decade, Obed had forgotten all about mushroom magic, buried it along with other useless mountain notions like bones stashed for a dead dog.

He needed to learn patience. If something came slowly, Obed would not wait around for it. That was a serious problem, because he lived in a terribly patient place. The steady mountain had always made him edgy, except, of course, when Danugun was still alive and their cupboard was forever full of pineos. Those mushrooms were her joy. With each bite, she tasted wonder and knew that she was loved by one of the last real, natural men alive, a man who shared with her the essence of a tree. Mushrooming was at the heart of their world. Her father, Fin Ohgma, had also learned mushroom secrets from his mother, Maeve, back in Ireland. All who practiced the secret, ancient art shared an understanding that bound them together like masons.

"Where there are amber mushrooms," Fin used to say, "the giants and little people are not far behind." Then his eyelids would swell up as he thought of home and the enchantments he was missing far across the Great Salt Sea.

Obed followed Nuda's jar of mushrooms back into the dining room. On the table, two painted baskets stood on the twins plates like twin towers, stalwart and foreboding, each filled with a square of carefully folded buckskin. Skeezucks longed to peek inside but he had been taught to wait his turn and ask for permission. Finally, Winay gave him the much-anticipated nod.

From within the buckskin, he retrieved a clear, triangular quartz stone with an eye. Neither candy nor an action game but a gift that was forever.

Tucked inside her basket, Aquinnee discovered Winay's gray stone pendant.

Nuda and Winay hugged one another and bit back tears. Cocheesee, swished lightly in Winay's hand, prompting Obed to raise up in acknowledgment of both the turtle shell rattle and the newfound standing of his children. Nuda touched each of the new Medicine People with the bear club. Neither flinched. Two good choices had been made.

Aquinnee pressed the pendant into her chest, "But I thought this was for . . ." the young woman's eyes widened.

"The next Yantuck Medicine Woman," Winay replied with her most knowing smile.

"But that would mean Skeezucks is . . ."

All three women gasped in unison.

Aquinnee snapped her head toward her brother. As their faces met, their hearts rang with joy. Ashneon's turquoise eyes stared at them, approvingly, from a photo hanging on the wall. Those eyes had always been their sea of comfort in stormy times.

Skeezucks surveyed his sister's twice-woven braids, a regal style befitting her new position. What a good thing he had let her braid his hair that morning. His stomach grew hollow; he missed Tomuck terribly. But now was definitely not the time to cry.

"We'll make them proud," he said. "Uh, excuse me a sec."

As Skeezucks flew up the stairs, each step hummed softly. He lifted the maple log from Tomuck's night stand, while a red-winged blackbird fidgeted on a branch beside the window sill. Sitting tall on the old man's stiff mattress, the young Medicine Chief whittled frantically, wiping tears onto his shirt collar.

Observe, concentrate, and remember.

If only he had paid a little better attention.

Aquinnee called Skeezucks back downstairs for a duet of Tamak Wigo (Tree Medicine), Tomuck's favorite song. Regimented music practice would continue to be a part of her life, because that is what Tomuck wanted. She might never see Carnegie Hall but she would be ready just in case.

"Gather 'round! Time for us to share some mushroom sandwiches with our two young oracles!" bellowed Nuda, fiercely commanding the universe with her cane.

Everybody liked that. Even Obed roared. Up at the museum, their laughter was echoed by the cackles of wooden baskets, masks, mortars, bowls, and spoons. A one-legged wooden man howled loudest of all.

It had been a very long while since Skeezucks had seen his father laugh. The moment he peered at him through the eye-stone, the boy knocked over the salt and pepper. There, in Obed's place, he spied a scraggly, one-legged wooden doll all dressed in green.

A limerick suddenly popped into Skeezuck's head:

There once was a stone with an eye
Through which all chosen spirits could spy
Without effort or task
It could rip any mask
Be it ruse, trick, deception, or lie.

There must be something about that doll in one of Winay 's old books—maybe even something about this stone.

But where had she put all those books, anyway?

And what ever happened to that guy, Peter, the one Ashneon claimed was such an expert on everything?

Skeezucks blinked a moment at the eyestone in his hand. Deep within it, he could just make out a woman flying. Was she one of those Oracles everyone was talking about?

Now that the Mockko twins were on their way, Nuda and Winay looked as though they could sleep for a hundred years. Aquinnee and Skeezucks were custom-made for the role of medicine. Carrying magic from both sides of the Atlantic, they were now the youngest of those elite recruits, that privileged cadre of time-honored wizards whose training and selection was the secret nub of all mountain activity.

"Winay, what do the triangles on this pendant mean?" asked Aquinnee.

"Those are mountains."

Deep lines rippled, like waves, across the young woman's forehead.

"So the person who wears this is part of the mountain or—?

"Or the one who cares for the mountain," Winay cut in. "At least until some other person or being comes along to look after it."

"But there can only be one real Medicine Woman and one Medicine Man, Winay, only one of each in charge."

"No. Only the Creator is in charge. And remember, there are always three. You will find three medicine people in every tribe. There are many protectors in the universe, many who hold a bit of magic, but at any given time there must be three in any given spot who are in their prime. Got to have three to perform a ceremony. Three is a magic number. After all, how many sides does a mountain have?"

Skeezucks cut in, "Wait, Winay. Then who is the . . ."

He was interrupted by a rhythmic knock at the door.

Winay turned toward the noise. "Excuse me, excuse me." *169*

She cut a pathway, waving the bear club before her like a scythe. "Be right there!" Skeezucks gasped, thinking Winay had suddenly been possessed by the spirit of Tomuck; she never rushed around like that.

At the front door stood a rusty-headed boy, the same one who had visited the museum some time ago and abruptly bolted. Although he seemed to have now grown a beard. Winay pulled herself up nearly straight.

"Soo, the time has coom," he said with a sniff.

"So it seems," she sniffed back. "Well, let's make the best of it. Shall we? It's for the good of one and all. You'll be needing this, I suppose?"

"Luvly, thank yew," he said, taking the bear club. "Ull be uf to see me Colleen now," he winked.

Winay tried so hard to shake away the image of the visitor that she appeared temporarily palsied.

"Winay!" called Aquinnee, running in from the next room. "Who was at the door?" The young woman poked her head outside and saw only the evening star peeking out from above an oak tree.

"Oh, just someone who wanted to see the museum. I told him we were closed till tomorrow. What did you need, birdie?"

"Just one more question, Winay." Aquinnee bounded toward the door, breathless. "If I wear this necklace, what will you carry?"

"Come. Look out the window, Quinnee. What do you see?"

"Not much. It's pretty cloudy tonight."

"Be patient and observe more carefully."

"Well there's one, no two, stars coming out, and oops you were right, there's more. Grandmother Moon has decided to show her face."

"All that you see, for as far as you can see—that is your celestial family. Your real family. Not just us foolish folks here on the mountain, but your true parents, grandparents, cousins and relatives back to the beginning. What more does anyone need to carry than the universe that surrounds us?"

"But here on the mountain, Winay, you are still the Medicine Woman and you still need to carry something powerful."

"Oh but I do. I do," she picked up Cocheesee. "Don't underestimate this little old turtle rattle." The old woman's eyes twinkled as she shook it. "Grandfather Turtle is everything. Once you have him, all things are possible. You do remember how the world began, don't you?"

NOTES ON CHARACTERS AND LANGUAGE

Author's Note: Many words have been translated or adapted from indigenous southern New England dialects using a loose orthography.

Aquinnee Mockko: daughter of Obed and Danugun
"Aquinnee" is a nickname for "Aquinnah," the ancient name of the Gay Head Indians of Martha's Vineyard off Cape Cod. This tribe passes on great stories of giants and little people from their area.

Ashneon Quay: Medicine-Woman-In-Training
Ashneon was a pseudonym used by the family of The Rev. Samson Occum, an eighteenth-century Mohegan Indian scholar and schoolteacher. Occum founded Native American literature and Dartmouth College. Later in life, he became disillusioned with books and academia.
The last name "Quay" alludes to the Algonquian farewell/ greeting "aquay" (hello) and "quay, quay" (goodbye).

Cocheesee: means "little old man" in Mohegan.

Danugun Mockko: Late wife of Obed
Danu is the name for the ancient Irish spirit who protects water and earth-magic.

Dr. Foxen Arber: New Light Psychiatrist

Foxen was an aide to seventeenth-century Mohegan Sachem, Uncas, who frequently spoke on the leader's behalf.

Dr. Peter Lymmel: Anthropologist

"Lymmel" is the Swedish word for "cad."

Fin Ohgma: Father of Danugun Mockko

Ohgma is the Irish spirit of wisdom. Fin is an ancient Irish hero, sometimes called a giant.

Hobbo: wooden spirit doll

Hobbomockko is the name of a dangerous spirit, residing in New England since memory.

John Mason:

John Mason was a seventeenth century American colonial captain. Along with John Underhill, he led the Mohegan and Narragansett tribes in a battle with the Pequot Indians in 1637. Mason directed those Native troops to burn the Pequot families out of their homes. Whether the Indians agreed to this, or not, is subject to historical speculation.

Muggs Mockko: Late husband of Nuda

A "Muggs Hole" is a root storage place, built of stones into the side of a hill. Here, it also alludes to a hiding place.

Nuda Mockko: Old Woman Fortune Teller

"Nuda" is short for "manuda," which derives from the same root as "Manitou," the word for both "Mystery" or "Spirit." "Mockko" refers to big medicine, usually of the negative kind.

Obed Mockko: Aspiring New Light Medicine Man, son of Nuda.
The words "obed mockko" and "Hobbomockko" translate
to mean "he is bad/dangerous."

Shamaquin Quay: Ashneon's late mother.
"Shamaquin" is a corruption of the words "Shaman" and
"aquin" (an Algonquian root).

Sigi Malinke: Spirit Woman
In Mali, Sigi is a ceremony relating to the Great Mask of the
Dead. The Malinke are a tribe in that area.

Skeezucks Mockko: son of Obed and Danugun
"Skeezucks" means "little eyes / squinty eyes," suggesting a
special kind of sight.

Sotona: ancient Judeo-Christian name for the devil
This name is found in the Book of Enoch, an ancient apoc-
ryphal text, preserved in Ethiopia. Its scriptures were widely
accepted by early Christians.

Tashteh Sook: Patuxet Medicine-Man-In-Training
"Tashteh Sook" was the name of a great Narragansett Indian
leader from colonial times. The men of that Tribe are known for
being tall and well-built.

Tomuck Weekum: Medicine Chief
"Tomuck" is a variant form of "Tamak" which means forest.
Anything with the prefix "wee," as in "Weegun," is good. "Tuck"
is reminiscent of Weetuck, an ancient southern New England
giant who lived in harmony with the Indians, but had some
difficulty getting along with other creatures.

West Wind Monroe: Wiccan Femme Fatale

In many Indian tribes, the "west wind" brings death and suggests passage into the spirit world.

Winay Weekum: Medicine Woman

"Winay" means old woman.

Wunneah Tatoon: Patuxet Beauty in love with Tashteh

"Wunneah" is short for Wunneanatsu, which means "one who is beautiful on the inside" according to Schaghticoke elder Trudie Lamb Richmond. Tatoon is a family name common to several southern New England Tribes including the Mohegan and Narragansett.

Yantuck:

"Yantuck" means people of the rushing water.